HIS BRAND
OF PASSION

HIS BRAND OF PASSION

BY

KATE HEWITT

First published in Great Britain 2013
by Mills & Boon, an imprint of Harlequin (UK) Limited.
Large Print edition 2013
Harlequin (UK) Limited, Eton House,
18-24 Paradise Road, Richmond, Surrey TW9 1SR

© Kate Hewitt 2013

ISBN: 978 0 263 23233 2

Harlequin (UK) policy is to use papers that are natural,
renewable and recyclable products and made from
wood grown in sustainable forests. The logging and
manufacturing process conform to the legal environmental
regulations of the country of origin.

Printed and bound in Great Britain
by CPI Antony Rowe, Chippenham, Wiltshire

To Zoe,
thanks for your inspiration and friendship,
love, K.

CHAPTER ONE

HE WAS CHECKING his *phone.*

Zoe Parker twitched with irritation as she watched the groom's best man thumb a few buttons on his smart phone. Discreetly, at least, but *honestly.* Her sister Millie and her husband-to-be Chase were saying their vows, and Aaron Bryant was texting.

He was unbelievable. He was also a complete jerk. A sexy jerk, unfortunately; tall, broad and exuding authority out of every pore. He also exuded a smug arrogance that made Zoe want to kick him in the shin. Or maybe a little higher. If she could have, she would have reached across the train of her sister's elegant cream wedding dress and snatched the mobile out of his fingers. Long, lean fingers with nicely square-cut nails, but who was noticing? She certainly wasn't.

She turned back to the minister, determinedly giving him her full attention. Maybe Aaron the Ass would pick up a few pointers. Honestly, the man was a gazillionaire and was a regularly attender at Manhattan's most elite social functions—did he really need a brush-up course on basic etiquette? Based on his behaviour since he'd strode into the rehearsal forty-five minutes late last night, clearly impatient and bored before he'd so much as said hello, Zoe was thinking yes.

She glanced at Millie, who thankfully had not noticed the phone. She looked beautiful, radiant in a way Zoe had never seen before, her eyes shining, her cheeks flushed. Everything about her was happy.

Zoe smothered the very tiny pang of something almost like envy. She wasn't looking for Mr Right. She'd gone for too many Mr Wrongs to think he existed, or to want to find him if he did. Although admittedly Millie's almost-husband was pretty close. Chase Bryant was charming, genuinely nice and *very* attractive.

Just like his brother.

Instinctively Zoe slid her gaze back to Aaron. He was still on the phone. Forget charming or nice but, yes, he was most definitely attractive. A faint frown creased his forehead and his lips thinned. He had nice lips, even pursed as they were in obvious irritation. They were full, sculpted, yet completely masculine too. In fact, everything about this irritating man was incredibly masculine, from the breadth of his shoulders to the near-black of his eyes and hair to the long, lean curve of his back and thigh…

'By the power vested in me, I now pronounce you husband and wife.'

Zoe yanked her gaze upwards from her rather leisurely perusal of Aaron Bryant's butt in time to see Millie and Chase kiss—and Aaron slide his phone back into the side pocket of his suit blazer.

Ass.

The congregation broke into spontaneous and joyous applause and Millie linked arms with Chase as she turned to leave the church. Aaron followed and, as maid of honour, Zoe had to accompany him up the aisle. She slid her arm through his, realising it was the first time she'd actually touched him since he'd breezed in too late to the rehearsal to practise going through the recessional together.

Now she was annoyingly conscious of the strength of his arm linked in hers, his powerful shoulder inches from her cheek—and her fingers inches from his pocket. With the phone.

Zoe didn't think too much about what she was

doing. On the pretext of adjusting her bridesmaid's dress, she slid her arm more securely in Aaron's and her fingers slipped into his pocket and curled round the phone.

Chase's other brother Luke and his fiancée Aurelie fell in step behind them and they processed out onto the church steps and the summer sunshine of Fifth Avenue. Aaron pulled away from her without so much as a glance, and in one fluid movement Zoe took the phone from his pocket and hid it in the folds of her dress.

Not that it mattered. To all intents and purposes, according to Aaron she'd ceased to exist. He was gazing at his brother as if he were a puzzle he didn't understand and absent-mindedly patting his pocket. His phoneless pocket.

Zoe took the opportunity to tuck the phone among the blossoms of her bouquet. A little judicious tugging of ribbon and lace, and you wouldn't even know it was there.

Not that Zoe even knew what she was going to do with Aaron Bryant's phone. She just wanted to see his face when he realised he didn't have it.

Apparently that moment wasn't going to be now, because someone approached him and he dropped his hand from his pocket and turned to talk to whatever schmoozy bigwig wanted to hear about Bryant Enterprises, blah, blah, blah. This was *so* not her crowd.

It was Millie's crowd, though, and it was certainly Chase's. Millie was marrying into the Bryant family, a trio of brothers who regularly made the tabloids and gossip pages. Aaron certainly did; when Zoe flicked through the mags during the slow periods at the coffee shop, she almost always saw a picture of him with some bodacious blonde. Judging from the way he'd dismissed her upon introduction last night with one swiftly eloquent head-to-toe perusal, skinny brunettes were not his type.

'Zoe, the photographer wants some shots of the wedding party.' Amanda, Zoe's mother, elegant if a little fraught in pale blue silk, hurried up to her. 'And I think Millie's train needs adjusting, darling. That's your job, you know.'

'Yes, Mum, I know.' This was the second time she'd been Millie's maid of honour. She might not be as organised as her sister—well, not even remotely—but she could handle her duties. She'd certainly given Millie a great hen party, at any rate.

Smiling at the memory of her uptight sister singing karaoke in the East Village, Zoe headed towards the wedding party assembled on the steps of the church. The photographer wanted them to walk two blocks to Central Park, and Chase looked like he'd rather relax with a beer.

'Come on, Chase,' Zoe said as she came to stand next to him. 'You'll be glad of the photos a couple of months from now. You and Millie can invite me over and have a slideshow.'

Chase's mouth quirked in a smile. 'I'm not sure who that would torture more.'

Zoe laughed softly and went to adjust Millie's aforementioned train. 'Has Mum sent you over here to fuss?' Millie guessed, and Zoe smiled.

'I never fuss.'

'That's true, I suppose,' Millie said teasingly and they started walking towards Central Park. 'You don't know the meaning of the word.'

An hour later the photos were over and Zoe was circulating through the opulent ballroom of The Plaza Hotel, a glass of champagne in hand. She'd been keeping an eye out for Aaron, because she still wanted to see his face when he realised he didn't have his phone. During the photos she'd taken the opportunity to remove the phone from her bouquet and put it in her clutch bag. The little luminous screen had glowed accusingly at her; there were eleven missed calls and eight new texts.

Clearly Aaron was a *very* important person. Was it a scorned lover begging him back, or some boring business? Either way, he could surely do without it for an hour or so.

It was easy enough to keep track of him in the crowded ballroom; he was a good two inches taller than any other man there, and even without the height his sense of authority and power had every female eye turning towards him longingly—and Zoe was pretty sure he knew it. He walked with the arrogant ease of someone who had never needed to look far for a date—or a willing bed partner.

Zoe's mouth twisted downwards. She really disliked this man, and they hadn't even had a conversation yet. But they surely would; they were seated next to each other at the wedding party's table. Although, come to think of it, Aaron seemed perfectly capable of ignoring someone seated next to him. He'd texted during a wedding ceremony, after all.

Smiling, she patted her bag. She looked forward to seeing the expression on his face when he realised he didn't have his phone—and she did.

Aaron Bryant surveyed the crowd with edgy impatience. How long would he have to stay? It was his brother's wedding, he knew, and he was best man—two compelling reasons to stay till the bitter end. On the other hand, he had a potential disaster brewing with some of his European investments and he knew he needed to keep close tabs on all the interested parties if Bryant Enterprises was going to weather this crisis. Automatically he slid his hand into his pocket where he kept his phone, only to remember with a flash of annoyance and a tiny needling of alarm that it was gone. He'd had it during the wedding, and he was never one to leave his phone anywhere. So where had it gone? A pickpocket on the way to Central Park? It was possible, he supposed, and very frustrating.

People had started moving towards the tables, and with a resigned sigh Aaron decided he'd stay at least through dinner. His phone, thankfully, was backed up on his computer, and he could access everything he needed at the office. It was password-protected, so he didn't need to worry about information leaks, and as soon as he got to the office he could put a trace on it. Still, he didn't like being without it. He was never without his phone, and too much was brewing for him not to be in touch with his clients for very long.

He approached the wedding-party table, steeling himself for an interminable hour or two. Millie and Chase were wrapped up in their own world, which he couldn't really fault, and his relationship with his brother Luke's fiancée Aurelie was, at best, awkward.

A few months ago he'd tried to intimidate her into leaving Luke, and it hadn't worked. He'd been trying to protect Luke and, if he were honest, Bryant Enterprises. Aurelie was a washed-up pop star whom the tabloids ridiculed on a daily basis, not someone Aaron had wanted associated with his family. Admittedly, she'd staged something of a comeback in the last year, but relations with both Luke and his fiancée were still rather strained.

He slid into his seat and offered both Luke and Aurelie a tight-lipped smile. He couldn't manage much more; his mind was buzzing with the stress of work and the half-dozen crises that were poised to explode into true chaos. A woman came to sit next to him and Aaron glanced at her without interest.

Zoe Parker, Millie's sister and maid of honour. He hadn't spoken to her last night or this morning, but he supposed he'd have to make some conversation over the meal. She was pretty enough, with wide grey eyes and long, dark hair, although her

skinny, sinewy figure wasn't generally his prefer-
ence. She glanced at him now, her lips curving in
a strangely knowing smile.

'How are things, Aaron? You don't mind if I call
you Aaron?'

'Of course not.' He forced a small smile back.
'We're practically family, after all.'

'Practically family,' she repeated thoughtfully.
'That's right.' She flicked her long, almost-black
hair over her shoulders and gave him another
smile. Flirtatious? No—knowing. Like she knew
something about him, some secret.

Absurd.

Dismissing her, Aaron turned to the walnut and
blue-cheese salad artfully arranged on the plate in
front of him. He'd just taken his first bite when he
heard a familiar buzz—an incoming text or voicemail. Instinctively he reached into his pocket, only
to silently curse. It couldn't be his phone that was
buzzing. He heard the sound again, and saw it was
coming from Zoe's lacy little clutch bag that she'd
left by the side of her plate.

He nodded towards it. 'I think your phone is
ringing.'

She glanced at him, eyebrows raised. 'I didn't
bring my phone.'

Aaron stared at her, completely nonplussed. 'Well,' he said, turning back to his salad, 'something's buzzing in your bag.'

'That sounds like an interesting euphemism.' Aaron didn't reply, although he felt a surprising little kick of something. Not lust, precisely; interest, perhaps, but no more than a flicker. 'Anyway,' she continued, her tone breezy, 'that's not *my* phone.'

There was something about the way she said it, so knowingly, so provocatively, that Aaron turned towards her sharply, suspicion hardening inside him. She smiled with saccharine sweetness, her eyes glinting with mischief.

'Whose phone is it, then?' Aaron asked pleasantly, or at least he hoped he sounded pleasant. This woman was starting to seriously annoy him.

Zoe wasn't able to reply for someone had tapped their fork against their wine glass and, with a round of cheers, Millie and Chase bowed to popular demand and kissed. Aaron turned back to his salad, determined to ignore her.

The phone buzzed again. Zoe made a tsking noise and reached for her bag. '*Someone* gets a lot of messages,' she said and, opening the little clutch, she took out his mobile.

The expression on Aaron Bryant's face was, Zoe

decided, priceless. His mouth had dropped open and he stared slack-jawed at the sight of his phone in her hand. She glanced at the screen, saw there were now fourteen texts and nine voicemails, and with a shake of her head she slipped it back into her bag.

She glanced back at Aaron and saw he'd recovered his composure. His eyes were narrowed to black slits, his mouth compressed into a very hard line. He looked as if he were carved from marble, hewn from granite—hard and unyielding and, yes, maybe even a little scary. But beautiful too, like a darkly terrifying angel.

Zoe felt her heart give a little tremor and she reached for her bread roll as if she hadn't a care in the world. 'Where,' Aaron asked in a low voice that thrummed through his chest and through Zoe, 'did you get that phone?'

She swallowed a piece of roll and smiled. 'Where do you think I got it?'

His eyes blazed dark fire as he glared at her. 'From my pocket.'

'Bingo.'

He shook his head slowly. 'So you're a thief.'

She tilted her head to one side as if considering his statement, although her heart was beating hard and adrenalin pumped through her. 'That's a bit harsh.'

'You *stole* my phone.'

'I prefer to think of it as borrowing.'

'Borrowing.'

She leaned forward, anger replacing any alarm she'd felt. 'Yes, *borrowing* it—for the duration of my sister and your brother's wedding reception. Because, no matter how much of a bigwig business tycoon you might be, Aaron Bryant, you don't text during a wedding ceremony. And I don't want you ruining this day for Millie and Chase.'

He stared at her, colour washing his high cheek-bones, his eyes glittering darkly. He was furious, utterly furious, and Zoe felt a little frisson of—fear? Maybe, but something else too. Something like excitement. Smiling, she patted her bag with the still-buzzing phone. Good Lord, he received a lot of calls. 'You can have it back after Millie and Chase leave for their honeymoon.'

Aaron's expression turned thunderous and he leaned forward, every taut line of his body radi-ating tightly leashed anger. 'I'll have it back now.'

'I don't think so.'

She saw him reach for the bag and quickly she

grabbed it and put it in her lap. Aaron arched an incredulous eyebrow.

'You think that's going to stop me?' he murmured, and it sounded almost seductive. Zoe felt a sudden, prickling awareness raise goosebumps all over her body. Before she could make any answer, Aaron slid his hand under the table. Zoe stiffened as she felt his hand slide along her thigh. The man was audacious, she had to give him that. Audacious and fearless.

She felt his fingers slide along her inner thigh, his palm warm through the thin silk of her dress. To her own annoyance and shame she could not keep a very basic and overwhelming desire from flooding through her, turning her insides warm and liquid. She shifted in her seat, and just as Aaron's hand reached the bag in her lap she slid the phone out of it.

'Give me that phone, Zoe.' His hand was clenched in her lap and, even though seduction had to be the last thing on his mind, Zoe could still feel her body's pulsing awareness of him. All he'd done was touch her leg. She had to get a grip and remember this was about the phone. Nothing else.

She raised her hand above the table, the phone still clutched in it, and slowly shook her head. 'No.'

Aaron's lips thinned. 'I could take it from you by force.'

She had no doubt he could. 'That would cause a scene.'

'You think I care?'

No, Zoe realised, she didn't think he did. Considering his behaviour so far, she didn't think he cared at all. She imagined him prying the phone from her hand. It would be like taking candy from a baby. She was no match for his strength, and she couldn't stand the thought of enduring Aaron's mocking triumph for the rest of the evening.

Impulsively, her gaze locked on Aaron's, she slid the phone down the front of her dress. He stared back at her and something flared in his eyes that made the awareness inside her pulse harder.

'That looks a little…strange,' he remarked, and Zoe glanced down to see her cleavage obscured by a bulky object in the middle of the dress. It did, indeed, look a bit strange.

'Easily fixed,' she replied breezily, and with a bit of pushing and pulling of the strapless dress she managed to get the phone to lie flat under the shelf of her breasts. Still a little strange, but not too bad. And totally impossible for Aaron to access.

He sat back in his chair, shook his head slowly. 'You really are a piece of work.'

'I'll take that as a compliment.'

'It wasn't meant as one.'

'Even so.'

He chuckled softly, the sound hard and without humour, and leaned forward again. 'You think,' he murmured, his voice stealing right inside her, 'I can't get that phone out of your dress?'

Zoe glanced at him, tried for haughty amusement. 'Not easily.'

'You have no idea what I'm capable of.'

'Actually, based on your behaviour so far, I think I have a fairly good idea of the level of boorishness you're willing to sink to,' she replied. 'But even you, I believe, would draw the line at mauling the maid of honour in the middle of a wedding reception.'

Aaron stared at her for a few seconds, his gaze flicking over her face, seeming to assess her. His face had turned blank, expressionless, which made Zoe uneasy. She couldn't read him at all. Then he shrugged and turned back to his meal. 'Fine,' he said, and he sounded completely bored, utterly dismissive. 'Give it back to me in a couple of hours.'

Zoe sat there, the phone hot and a little sweaty

against her chest, and felt weirdly deflated. She'd enjoyed sparring with him, she realised. It had been invigorating and, yes, a tiny bit flirtatious. But, based on the way Aaron was now focused completely on his salad, she was now the furthest thing from his thoughts. Well, she thought with a sigh, wriggling a little to make herself a bit more comfortable with a phone inside her dress, at least she'd taught him a lesson.

Aaron knew about patience. It was a lesson he'd learned from childhood, when his father would summon him to his study only to make him wait standing by the door for an hour or more, while he concluded some trivial piece of business.

It was a lesson he'd needed, for it had taken patience to rebuild Bryant Enterprises from the ground up when his father had left it to him fifteen years ago, utterly bankrupt.

It was a lesson he would use now, for he knew it was only a matter of time before he found an opportunity to corner Zoe and get his phone back.

He had to admire her bravado and tenacity, even if the whole exercise annoyed the hell out of him. She was different from most women he knew, utterly uninterested in impressing him. In fact, she seemed to want the opposite: to aggravate him. Well, it was working.

An hour into the festivities Zoe excused herself from the table. Aaron watched her head to the ladies' room with narrowed eyes. He waited a few seconds before he excused himself and followed her out of the ballroom.

The ladies' room was one of those ridiculously feminine boudoirs, complete with spindly little chairs and embroidered tissue boxes. Aaron slipped inside and put a finger to his lips when an elderly matron applying some garishly bright coral lipstick stared at him in shock.

'I want to surprise my girlfriend,' he whispered, and then mimed getting down on one knee as if in a marriage proposal. The woman's face suffused with colour to match her mouth and she bobbed her head in understanding before hurrying outside.

He was alone with Zoe.

He heard the toilet flush and stepped back so she couldn't see him as she came out of the stall. He watched as she moved to the sink and washed her hands, humming under her breath. He took the opportunity to admire her figure, skinny though it was. She had some nice curves, highlighted by how they were encased in tight pink silk. A very nice bottom, as a matter of fact, and long, lean legs. He didn't usually pay attention to the backside of a woman, but standing behind Zoe he found his gaze riveted—and his body responding in the most elemental way.

Then she looked up, and her eyes widened as she caught sight of him in the mirror just a few feet behind her, lurking like a dark shadow.

'Hello, Zoe.'

She turned around slowly, drying her hands. 'This *is* the ladies' room, you know,' she remarked, and to her credit she sounded as light and wry as ever.

'I know.'

'What are you doing here?'

He took a step towards her and was gratified to see her eyes widen a little more. She *should* be afraid of him. Or, if not afraid, then at least a little wary. 'What do you think I'm doing here? I want my phone.'

She crossed her arms over her chest. 'Sorry, Bryant. You'll have to wait until the reception is over.'

'I don't think so.'

Her lips parted and he saw something flare in her eyes. Fear? No, it was excitement. He felt it himself, a surprising little pulse of anticipation.

She was so not his type, and yet in that moment he knew he was quite looking forward to putting his hand down her dress.

'And how,' she asked, her voice turning husky, 'do you think you're going to get it back?'

'Quite easily.' He took another step towards her, so she was pressed against the sink, her head angled up towards him. She didn't move, didn't even try to escape him. Was she wondering if he'd dare do it? Or did she want him to? As much as he did, perhaps.

His gaze fastened on hers, and something pulsed and blazed between them. Aaron felt it, felt the very air seem to tauten around them, crackle with the sudden, electric energy they had created. Slowly, deliberately, he reached out and slid a few fingers down the bodice of her dress. Her skin was silky and warm, the sides of her breasts brushing his fingers. Zoe gasped aloud. Aaron smiled even as desire arrowed through him. 'Quite a tight fit.'

'Quite,' she managed.

With the tip of his fingers he could just touch his phone, but there was no way he could actually get it. Not without unzipping the dress completely… which was a possibility. Anything felt possible right now.

'You are outrageous,' Zoe gasped, and Aaron chuckled softly.

'I'm not the one who started this, sweetheart.'

'Yes, you did. When you texted—'

He was stroking the sides of her breasts with his fingers in an attempt to reach the phone and Aaron knew that neither of them was immune. He saw Zoe's pupils dilate with desire and felt himself harden even more.

He slid his hand lower.

'You're not going to get it,' Zoe said breathlessly, and Aaron arched an eyebrow.

'One way or another, I'll get it.'

'I don't think so,' she answered, her tone mocking his perfectly. He almost laughed. His fingertip brushed the phone and then, to his annoyance, the damn thing slid lower so it was resting against her stomach. There was no way he could get it now.

Unless…

'Don't you dare,' Zoe whispered and Aaron smiled.

'I think this whole encounter is about daring, don't you?' He removed his hand from her dress, allowing his fingers to stroke her soft, small breasts on the way up. Zoe stared at him, pupils still dilated, lips parted, her breath coming in little pants.

'You wouldn't.'

'Want to bet?'

And, with his gaze still hard on hers, he put his hand up under her skirt.

Zoe stood rigid, unable to believe Aaron Bryant had just put his hand up her dress. And he'd already put it down her dress. Her whole body felt as if it were on fire from those few, calculated little touches. She was hopeless. Hopelessly attracted to this arrogant ass of a man.

So much so that she didn't even move as his hand slid up her thigh, his fingers warm and seeking on her bare flesh. His gaze was riveted on hers, and she knew, no matter how angry or determined he was, he felt something for her. She could feel the attraction between them, heavy and thick. His hand slid higher, smoothing along her hip before he finally found the phone with his fingers and tugged it down. And she hadn't resisted at all, not even the tiniest bit.

'I can't believe you,' she whispered and he smiled.

'Believe it.' He slid his hand lower to the juncture of her thighs, the phone in his palm. Zoe's breath came out in a devastated rush as he pressed his hand against her, the phone still in it, cool against her heated and tender flesh. Sensation sizzled straight through her and she sagged against the counter.

'You are incredible.'

'Why, thank you.' He pressed again and she closed her eyes, feeling utterly exposed and shameless, yet helpless to prevent it.

'It wasn't a compliment,' she managed, and he laughed softly.

'Considering the response I'm coaxing from you, I rather think it was.'

Zoe opened her eyes, forced herself to straighten. 'What I really meant is that you're incorrigible.'

'True.' His hand was still between her legs, teasing her, tormenting her. It took all her effort to remain still, not to allow her body to invite his deeper caresses. 'But then so are you.' He stared at her for a long moment, and then with one last press of his hand he stepped away. 'Thanks for my phone,' he said, and then he was gone.

Aaron stalked from the bathroom, his whole body blazing with unfulfilled desire. He had not expected that to happen, for that skinny, seriously annoying woman to awaken in him such a fierce need. Well, she had, and it was going to be incredibly difficult to focus on work as he needed to.

Swearing under his breath, he found a private alcove in the ballroom and checked his messages and texts. Just as he'd thought, the European market was imploding and his investors were panicking. He spent thirty minutes doing damage control and then he slid his phone back into his pocket.

He stared into space for a few minutes, felt the familiar cold wash of fear sweep through him. He hated these close calls. Hated feeling, as he'd felt for fifteen years, like Bryant Enterprises was about to slip out of his grasp even as it remained the chain that bound and choked him.

How much had those few hours without his phone cost him? It was impossible to measure, yet Aaron knew there was a cost. There always had been, always would be. And with a sudden, cold certainty, he also knew who was going to pay this time.

He strode back into the reception and saw that things were starting to wind down. Chase and Millie were coming out in their going-away clothes for a week's honeymoon on St Julian's, the Bryants' private island in the Caribbean. Zoe stood behind her sister, smiling, although Aaron thought she looked rather wistful, maybe even sad. She hardly seemed like the type to want a ring on her finger, but who knew? Most women wanted one. Wanted the ridiculous fairy tale, the impossible dream.

He waited until Chase and Millie had left and the other guests were starting to trickle away. He said goodbye to Luke and Aurelie, managing a few minutes' stilted conversation, before he went in search of Zoe.

She was standing by their table, picking some bits of confetti out of her bouquet. Her hair streamed over her shoulders in a dark ribbon, her body lithe and slender, and Aaron remembered just how silky and warm her skin had felt, how her body had helplessly yielded to his.

He strode towards her. She glanced up at him, and he felt her tense, her eyes dark with shadows. 'What do you want now?'

'You,' he said flatly, and her jaw dropped.

'What—?'

'I have a limo waiting outside.'

She stared at him in disbelief and Aaron wondered in a detached sort of way if she'd refuse. He'd felt her response earlier, the heat and the strength of it. He was pretty sure she'd felt his own. If she refused, she had more scruples—or at least more self-control—than he'd credited her with.

Wordlessly Zoe tossed her bouquet back on the table. 'Let's go,' she said and, with a smile of triumph curling his mouth, Aaron led her out of the ballroom.

CHAPTER TWO

She didn't do stuff like this—one-night stands, flings with strangers. It was crazy. *She* was crazy, Zoe thought as she followed Aaron outside into the warm summer air and then straight into the luxurious leather interior of the limo that was waiting by the kerb, just as he'd said.

What on earth had made her agree? She didn't even like him. But she was incredibly, irresistibly attracted to him. And, Zoe realised with a sudden flash of insight, the fact that she didn't like him made this whole encounter emotionally safe. Aaron Bryant was no danger to her already battle-worn heart. Even if this whole scenario was way outside her comfort zone.

'Where are we going?' she asked as the limo pulled away from the Plaza.

'My apartment.'

She nodded, felt a little frisson of something close to fear. This was so not her. She might give off that reckless, devil-may-care attitude, but in her relationships she'd been depressingly, boringly conservative. And she'd got hurt time and time again as a result.

Maybe this *was* the way to go.

'Nervous?' Aaron asked, the word mocking, and Zoe just shrugged.

'Going home with a strange man to his apartment is a little out of the usual for me, no matter what you might think. But, considering how well-known you are, I think I'm pretty safe.'

Aaron stretched his arms out along the seat, his fingers just brushing her shoulder. Zoe resisted the urge to shiver under that thoughtless touch. 'How do you reckon that?' he asked.

'I don't think,' Zoe said, 'you want any bad publicity.'

He frowned, his eyes narrowing, before his wonderfully mobile mouth suddenly curved into a surprising smile. 'Are you actually threatening me?'

'Not at all. Just stating facts. And in any case, like you said earlier, we're practically family. It's hard to believe you're related to Chase, but since you are I'll assume you're not a complete psycho.'

'Thanks very much for that vote of confidence,' Aaron said dryly. He turned to gaze out of the window. 'Why is it hard to believe I'm related to Chase?'

Zoe shrugged. 'Mainly because he's actually nice.'

'I see.' He didn't seem at all offended, more amused. Zoe glanced out of the window at the cars and taxis streaming by in a blur. 'So where is your apartment, exactly?'

'We're here.'

'Here' was a luxury high-rise on West End Avenue, and Aaron's apartment was, unsurprisingly, the penthouse. The lift doors opened right into the living area, and Zoe stepped into a temple of modern design with floor-to-ceiling windows on three sides overlooking the city and the Hudson River.

'Nice,' she remarked, taking in the black leather sofas, the chrome-and-glass coffee table, the modern sculpture, and the white faux fur rug. A granite-and-marble kitchen opened onto a dining area with an ebony table that seated twelve. Everything was spotless, empty, barren. The place, Zoe decided, had no soul. Just like the man.

She walked to the window overlooking the Hudson, the inky-black river glimmering with lights. She felt Aaron approach from behind her, and then she shivered as he moved her hair and brushed his lips across the bared nape of her neck.

His hands fastened on her hips and then slid slowly upwards over the silk of her dress to cup her breasts. Zoe shivered again and then, with effort, stepped away.

'I don't know what impression you've formed of me, but I like a little conversation along with the sex.' She spoke lightly, even though she felt a tremble deep inside. She'd had plenty of boyfriends, but she'd never done this before, and never with a man like Aaron. Powerful. Overwhelming. A little…frightening.

'Conversation?' Aaron repeated, sounding completely nonplussed. 'What do you want to talk about? The latest film? The weather?'

'I think you could do better than that,' she answered tartly. 'And, actually, what I'd really like to talk about is food.'

Aaron arched one dark eyebrow, unsmiling. 'Food.'

'I'm hungry. Starving, actually. I never eat at parties.'

He simply stared and Zoe almost laughed. At least she felt a little easing of the tension coiling tighter and tighter inside her. She doubted Aaron was used to women who did anything more than nibble at the occasional lettuce leaf and take their clothes off on his command. She was determined to be different.

'I don't have any food,' he said after a moment, his gaze still hard and assessing on her. 'I always order in or eat out.'

'Perfect,' Zoe replied breezily. 'We can order in.'

He still looked nonplussed, frankly incredulous. 'What do you want to order?'

'A California roll.'

'Sushi?'

'If by sushi you mean the non-raw fish kind, then yes.' She was inexplicably gratified to see his mouth curve in the tiniest of smiles.

'If we're going to order sushi, we'll do it properly,' he said and slid his phone out of his pocket.

Zoe smiled. 'At last you're putting your phone to good use.'

This woman drove him crazy. In far too many ways. His palms itched to touch her, yet here she was insisting they order *sushi,* as if they were some couple about to have a quiet night in. He'd almost asked her if she wanted to rent a DVD while they were at it, but then he decided not to risk it. She might take him seriously.

The women he knew—and, more importantly, the women he went to bed with—didn't behave the way Zoe Parker did, which begged the question why he'd brought her back here in the first place.

He was used to women going along exactly with what he wanted. What he commanded. Hell, everyone did. He didn't allow for anything else.

And yet here he was, ordering her damn food. Still, he *was* hungry. He hadn't eaten much at the reception either, and he was willing to go along with Zoe's crazy ideas—to a point. Eventually and inevitably she would have to understand and accept who was calling the shots.

He slid his phone back into his pocket. 'The food should be here in about fifteen minutes.'

A flirty, cat-like smile played around her mouth. 'So what should we talk about for fifteen minutes?' she asked, and he could tell from her tone that she was laughing at him, that she knew the thought of making conversation for that long exasperated and annoyed him.

He didn't want to *talk*.

'I have no idea,' he said shortly, and her smile widened.

'Oh, I've got plenty of ideas, don't worry.' She walked over to the sofa and stretched out, her legs long and slim in front of her, her arms along the back. 'Let's see… We could talk about why you live in such an awful apartment.'

'Awful apartment?' he repeated in disbelief and she smiled breezily.

'I've been in morgues with more warmth. Or we could talk about how you don't get along with anyone in your family, or why you're so obsessive about work.' She batted her eyelashes. 'Are you compensating for something else, do you think?'

'Or,' he growled, 'we could both shut up and get on with what we came here for.'

'Now, that's a come-on I haven't heard before. Really charming. Makes me want to strip naked right now.'

Fury pulsed through him. He'd never met a woman who dished it out so much before. Most women wanted to impress him. He took a step towards her. 'A few hours ago you were practically melting in a puddle at my feet. I don't think I have much to worry about there, sweetheart.'

Her eyes flashed silver. 'Honestly, you are the most arrogant ass of a man I have ever met. I'm amazed there's enough room in this apartment for you, me and your ego.'

He stared at her, disbelief making his mind go blank. No one talked to him like this. *No one.* Zoe's mouth curled into a saccharine smile.

'I suppose no one has dared to tell you that before?' She didn't wait for an answer. 'I think Millie and Chase will be happy together, don't you?' Her eyes danced as she posed the question oh, so innocently and Aaron gritted his teeth. As if he wanted to talk about weddings, marriages and happy endings. He didn't want any of it, at least not for himself.

'I suppose so,' he said in a bored voice. 'I haven't really given it much thought.'

'What a surprise.'

'Why do you want to talk to me, anyway?' he asked. He hated the way she made him feel as if he'd lost control, and he was determined to get it back—however he could. 'You obviously don't like me, or anything about me. So what's there to chat about, really, Zoe?' He spread his hands wide, his eyebrows raised in challenge. For a moment she didn't answer and he felt a surge of triumph. *Gotcha.*

'Well,' she finally said, her mouth curving upwards once more, 'I always live in hope. No one's irredeemable, surely? Not even you.'

'What a compliment.'

'It wasn't meant to be one,' she answered, and he knew she was intentionally parroting what he'd said to her earlier. She eyed him mischievously. 'But take it as one, if you like.'

'I'm not interested in anything you say,' Aaron snapped. 'Compliments or otherwise. I think we've talked enough.'

'We're still waiting for the sushi,' Zoe reminded him and Aaron nearly cursed.

He shouldn't have ordered the damn sushi. He shouldn't have gone for any of this, he realised. The moment Zoe had slipped out of his arms and stopped playing by his rules he should have shown her the door. So why hadn't he?

Because he wanted her too much. And because not having her felt like losing. They'd been locked in a battle from the moment she'd taken his phone, and Aaron knew only one way of assuring sweet, sweet victory.

'I think we can make good use of the time while we wait,' he said, his voice deepening to a purr, and with a savage satisfaction he saw awareness—and perhaps alarm—flare in her eyes.

'I'm sure we could.' She crossed her legs. 'So were any of those messages on your phone actually important?'

'Critical,' Aaron informed her silkily. He loosened the knot of his ascot and saw how her gaze was drawn to the movement. 'Absolutely crucial.'

She pursed her lips. 'Oh, dear.'

'Considering all the inconvenience you put me to, I think you owe me.'

She raised her eyebrows. 'Owe you?'

'Definitely.' He shed his tie and unbuttoned the top few buttons of his shirt. 'And I can think of several ways you can pay me back.'

'Oh, I'm sure you could.' Her eyes narrowed as if she wanted to argue, but he saw the rapid rise and fall of her chest and knew she was affected. As affected as he was… Hell, he'd been in a painful state of arousal since she'd first slid into his limo.

The intercom buzzed, and the tension that had been coiling and tautening between them was, for the moment, broken. Aaron strode towards the door and buzzed the delivery man up, conscious of Zoe; she'd risen from the sofa and was wandering around the living room, glancing at a few of the paintings on the walls, her body like a lithe shadow as she moved through the darkened room.

She turned and joined him at the door, and he breathed in the scent of her, some soap or shampoo that smelled like vanilla. The ends of her hair brushed his shoulder. 'So what kind of sushi did you order, anyway?'

'The real kind.' Not that he had any interest in eating anything. The doorbell rang and he dealt with the delivery man before turning back to her. 'And you have to try some before I give you your California roll.'

'Oh, do I?' Her eyes glinted and she looked intrigued, maybe even a little confused. Hell, he was. Why was he playing this game? Why didn't he toss her the food, tell her to eat and then take her to bed? Even if that did have a touch of the Neanderthal about it, it was still more his style. Yet some part of him actually enjoyed their sparring. It invigorated him, at least and, even if taking her to bed would be the simpler and more expedient option, he wasn't quite ready to let go of all the rest.

He grabbed some plates and glasses and a bottle of wine from the kitchen and took it all over to the living area. After a second's pause he put it all on the coffee table and stretched out on the rug. Everything felt awkward, unfamiliar. He didn't do this. He didn't socialise with the women he slept with, he didn't *romance* them.

Zoe sat down next to him, a willing pupil. 'So what am I going to try first?'

'We'll start gently. Futomaki.'

'Which is?'

'Cucumber, bamboo shoots and tuna.'

She wrinkled her nose. 'Okay.'

Aaron handed her a roll and took one himself. Then he opened the wine and poured them both glasses. 'Cheers.'

'Cheers.' She took a sip of wine and a small bite of the sushi roll.

'Well?'

'It's okay. I can taste the tuna, though.'

He laughed, the sound strangely rusty. 'You don't like fish?'

'Not particularly.'

'Well, I admire your willingness to try.' He bit into his own roll, surprised and discomfited at how he was almost—almost—enjoying himself. Relaxing, even, which was ridiculous. He didn't do either—enjoyment or relaxation. He worked. He strove. Sometimes he slept.

'I admire your willingness to try too,' Zoe said, and Aaron glanced at her sharply.

'What do you mean?'

'I sense this is outside of your comfort zone,' she said, a hint of laughter in her voice. 'I imagine the women you take to bed go directly there, do not pass go, do not collect two hundred dollars.' She arched an eyebrow. 'They don't sit on your rug, drinking wine and eating sushi.'

He stilled, feeling weirdly, terribly exposed and even angry. 'No, they don't.'

'Sorry not to fall in step with your plans.' She didn't sound remotely sorry.

'I can be flexible on occasion.'

'How encouraging.'

'Try this one.' He handed her another sushi roll. Zoe stared at it in distaste.

'What is this?'

'Narezushi. Gutted fish in vinegar, pickled for at least six months.'

'You've got to be kidding me.'

'I don't make jokes.'

'Ever?'

He considered. 'Pretty much.'

She put the roll aside, shaking her head, her lips pursed and her eyes glinting. 'Why, Aaron, I almost feel sorry for you.'

'Don't,' he said roughly, the word a warning.

'Don't what?'

'Don't even think about feeling sorry for me.' No one did. No one should. He had everything he'd ever wanted, everything anyone wanted. He didn't need Zoe Parker's pity.

She laughed softly. 'Touched a sore spot, did I?'

He saw now that with the wine and the food she was getting over-confident. Presumptuous. Thinking that this meant something, that they were creating some kind of intimate situation here. It was time to start calling the shots, Aaron decided. And to let Zoe know the only kind of *intimate* he was interested in.

She was annoying him, Zoe knew. Making him angry. Shame, because for a little while there things had almost seemed pleasant. Aaron had almost seemed…normal.

And she liked baiting him. She needed to do it, because the intensity of her attraction—and her emotion—scared her. She didn't do intense, not anymore. Teasing him defused that, at least a little.

Except now the very air felt thick with tension, with desire. She saw his dark eyes flare darker and he set his plate and glass aside as Zoe braced herself, knowing the pleasant little interlude was over. Aaron Bryant was ready to get down to business.

She met his gaze, determined to stay insouciant, never to let him know how much he affected her. How much power he had over her. 'Party over?'

'I wouldn't say that.' He reached out one powerful hand and closed it around her wrist, pulling her slowly and inexorably towards him. Zoe didn't resist. She couldn't; already she felt that heavy languor steal through her veins, take over her brain. She was just way too attracted to this man. 'I'd say it's just beginning.'

Aaron pulled her onto his sprawled thighs, his hands on her hips so she was straddling him. She felt the press of his erection against the juncture of her own thighs and pleasure bolted straight through her. It took all her will-power not to press back, not to admit with her body how much she wanted him. She needed to keep some kind of pride. Some kind of defence.

'A different kind of party,' Aaron murmured and slid his hands up along her hips and waist to cup her breasts only briefly and then frame her face. He brought her forward to brush his lips against hers, and distantly Zoe realised this was the first time they'd kissed.

It started gently but within seconds it flamed into something else entirely—something deep, primal and urgent. His tongue slid inside the warmth of her mouth and his hips rocked against hers—and so much for her pride, because she rocked back helplessly, her body taking over, already desperately seeking release.

His hands slid back down to her waist, and then to her thighs, and he edged the dress over her bottom so it was rucked about her waist. She was bare below except for a skimpy thong. He slid his fingers along the silky length of her thigh to the heat of her. 'No phones here,' he murmured, and Zoe would have laughed except he was kissing her again. His fingers were working deft magic, and all she could think about was how much she wanted this.

In one easy movement Aaron rolled her onto her back so she was splayed out on the fur rug, her dress still around her waist. Aaron lay poised over her, his cheeks faintly flushed, his eyes gleaming with desire, his breath a little ragged. He looked beautiful, dark and powerful and he stole Zoe's breath away.

He tugged down the zip of her dress and in just a few seconds it was gone, tossed to the side of the room. Zoe stared up at him, wearing only a strapless bra and matching thong, wondering what Aaron Bryant would do with her now. Willing him to do just about anything.

'I'm amazed you managed to fit a phone in here at all,' he said, and ran his hand between her breasts, along her stomach, then dipping once more between her thighs. Zoe arched helplessly against his hand, and Aaron slid her panties off her. The bra followed soon after.

She lay there, naked and supine on the rug, every sense spinning into aching awareness. She supposed, distantly, that she should feel bare, exposed, nervous, but she felt none of that. All she felt was a glorious anticipation, an unbearable readiness. Aaron bent his head to her and his hands, lips and tongue seemed to be everywhere at once, teasing, tasting, tormenting her.

She tangled her hands in his hair, surprised by its softness, for everything else about him was so hard: eyes, mouth, body, attitude. *Heart.* But his hair was soft and she ran her fingers through it, glorying in it even as she arched and writhed beneath him, as his mouth and hands brought her to the brink of that pleasurable precipice again and again.

And then, with a quick rustle of foil, he slid on a condom and drove inside her in one single stroke. He lay suspended above her, braced on his fore-arms, his body fully inside hers. For one breathless moment he gazed down at her, his eyes blazing dark fire, and Zoe felt something in her lurch, shift. She saw need and something deeper flare in Aaron's eyes, and for a second this seemed like more than sex.

Then he started to move and she wrapped her legs around his waist to bring him even closer. The moment became one of raw, primal passion, and then one of endless pleasure.

When it was over Aaron rolled onto his back and Zoe lay there, spent and breathless, her mind spinning for a few glorious minutes before she returned to earth with a dull thud. The party was over, she knew, and she didn't relish being dismissed now that she'd served her purpose. She was pretty sure that was how Aaron treated his women, at least his one-night stands, of which she was most assuredly one. Surreptitiously she rolled over and reached for her discarded underwear, only to have Aaron stay her arm.

'Where do you think you're going?'

'I need to get going,' Zoe answered, keeping her voice light. 'Not that the sushi wasn't delicious.'

Aaron let out a low rumble of laughter, surprising her. For a man who didn't joke, he'd still managed to laugh twice this evening, a thought which absurdly pleased her. What did she care if he laughed?

'Not so fast,' he said and pulled her towards him. Her body instinctively slid around his, her soft places finding his hard ones, so they fit like two pieces of a puzzle. 'We need to find my bed.'

She felt a thrill at his gruffly spoken words, a ridiculous, huge thrill. He wanted her to stay? She hesitated, knowing the better, safer thing to do would be to leave. She knew herself, knew her weaknesses. Sex was sex to a man like Aaron, but to her it was something else. No matter what her head dictated, she couldn't keep her heart from always insisting this was the one, this was love. And already she sensed that she would fall harder and longer for a man like Aaron than any of the other men she'd known. Feeling anything but basic, primal lust for Aaron Bryant bordered on the utterly insane.

'Well, actually....' she began, and that was as far as she got. Aaron was smoothing his hands over her bottom, as if he were touching a rare silk, then his fingers slid between her legs and she gave up the battle she hadn't really been fighting. 'You have a bed?' she managed, and with a throaty chuckle—his third laugh—he scooped her up in his arms and carried her to his bedroom and his wonderful, king-sized bed.

Hours later Zoe lay in that bed with dawn's first pale fingers streaking across the city sky and watched Aaron sleep. She was exhausted, totally sated, and as she looked at him she felt a little dart of sorrow arrow inside her. She didn't regret this night; it had been too amazing for that. But as she looked at his face softened with sleep, his lashes feathering his cheeks and his softly sculpted lips slightly parted, she wished things could be different. That Aaron was a different kind of man.

Don't, she warned herself. *Don't do it again. Don't insist you're in love with a complete ass.* She'd only done that about four times before. Millie always teased her about the emotional toe-rags she dated, and Zoe usually laughed it off. After all, it was true. But that didn't make it hurt less.

Silently she slipped from the bed and went in search of her clothes. The last of the moonlight spilled into the living room, bathing the chrome and glass with a pearly sheen even as the horizon pinkened with the promise of a new day. Zoe dressed quickly and, with one last bittersweet glance towards the bedroom, she left.

Three weeks later Zoe had done her best to forget that incredible night with Aaron Bryant, although she couldn't keep herself from surreptitiously scanning the headlines of the tabloids and gossip magazines for a glimpse of his name. She saw a photograph of him at a movie premier with a gorgeous B-list actress and felt something inside her tighten, twist. Surely not jealousy? she asked herself. It would be incredibly, criminally stupid to be jealous. Aaron Bryant meant nothing to her, and she obviously meant nothing to him. Their one night, fantastic as it had been, was over.

Resolutely she went to work at The Daisy Café, a funky, independent coffee shop in Greenwich Village where she worked part-time as a barista. She went to the community centre where she worked afternoons as an art therapist, and tried to keep away from the tabloids.

One afternoon in early September she was working at the café when the smell of the coffee beans nearly made her lose her breakfast.

'I must be coming down with something,' she told Violet, her co-worker, a young woman of nineteen who had multiple piercings and hair dyed like her name. 'The smell of coffee is making me sick.'

Violet raised her eyebrows. 'If I don't know better, I'd think you were pregnant.' Zoe just stared at her, all the blood draining from her face, and Violet pursed her lips. 'Uh-oh.'

As soon as her shift ended Zoe bought a pregnancy test, telling herself she was being ridiculous. Aaron had used protection, after all. She probably just had some kind of stomach flu, but just to be safe…

She took the test in the tiny bathroom of her studio apartment, sitting on the edge of the tub while she watched two pink lines blaze across the little screen.

Pregnant.

She sat there, the test in hand, utterly in shock and completely numb. Yet as that blankness wore off she probed the emotion underneath like a sore tooth or a fresh scar and realised, to her surprise, it wasn't dismay or fear that she felt. It was almost… excitement. Happiness.

She shook her head, incredulous at her own emotions. A *baby*. The baby of a man she barely knew, didn't even like. And yet…a baby. A child, her child, already nestled inside her, starting to grow. She pressed one hand against her still-flat tummy in a kind of dazed incredulity.

She wanted this baby. Despite all the challenges and difficulties of being a single mother on a small salary, she wanted to have this child. She was thirty-one years old, and a happy-ever-after wasn't likely to be in her future. This was her chance to be a mother, a chance to find her own kind of happiness. And, even though the baby was no more than the size of a bean, it was *there*. And she wanted to nurture that tiny life, that part of her.

Over the next few days she wished she had someone to talk to, but none of her friends were remotely interested in pregnancy or babies, and ever since Millie had lost her husband and young daughter three years ago Zoe hadn't felt like she could burden her with her problems—and certainly not this. Children were still a no-go area for Millie.

There was, Zoe knew, at least one person she needed to talk to. Aaron, no matter how hands-off he intended to be—and, frankly, she hoped that was considerable—still needed to know he was going to be a father. Zoe didn't relish that conversation, but it didn't appear to be one she was going to have any time soon, for every time she called Bryant Enterprises and asked for Aaron she was put off by a prissy-sounding secretary.

She left message after message with her name and number, but a week went by of her calling every day and he never phoned back. Annoyed, she considered not telling him at all, but she knew she could never keep such a devastating secret. And, in any case, that kind of lie of omission would likely come back and bite her. Which left one other option, she decided grimly.

It didn't take too much effort to get Aaron's mobile number from Chase on a rather flimsy pretext of needing sponsors for a charity event she was supposed to be coordinating for the community centre, but when she tried his mobile he didn't answer that either. Jerk.

Ten days after she'd first taken the test Zoe resorted to a text message, which seemed appropriate, considering how a phone had figured in their first encounter.

Grimly she typed in the four words she'd decided would convey her situation to her baby's father:

I'm pregnant, you ass.

CHAPTER THREE

AARON STARED AT the text message in disbelief. He knew who it was from, even though the number wasn't one he recognised. Rather unusually, he'd only slept with one woman in the last month and, more significantly, he knew only one woman who would text him such a provocative message.

Zoe.

Pregnant?

Impossible. He'd used protection every time. Aaron stared at the text message, his eyes narrowing. He hadn't thought Zoe Parker a grasping gold-digger, but he supposed anything was possible. He'd certainly known women to reach for flimsy pretexts in an attempt to ensnare him.

In any case, this was something he could nip in the bud very easily. Frowning, he tossed his phone aside and turned to his laptop. It shouldn't be too difficult to find out where Zoe worked and lived.

Late that morning Aaron was standing in front

of The Daisy Café, patrons spilling out into the September sunshine, holding their vente lattes and chai teas. Aaron could see Zoe behind the curved counter, working the espresso machine. Her hair was back in a neat ponytail, and she wore a tight black T-shirt that reminded him rather uncomfortably of what she'd looked and felt like underneath.

Pushing that unhelpful thought away with an impatient sigh, he headed inside. Heads turned as soon as he entered. At six feet four with the shoulders of a linebacker, Aaron often caught stares. Some people recognised him, and a woman he didn't know started to shimmy towards him, a calculating hope in her eyes. Aaron headed for the counter.

'Zoe.'

She looked up, her grey eyes widening as she took in his presence in the little café. Then her mouth twisted in a sardonic smile and she put her hands on her hips.

'Well, well, you finally got my message.'

'Finally?'

'I've only been trying to call you for a week.'

Aaron just shrugged. As far as he was concerned their one night had ended at dawn, when she'd snuck out of bed before he could show her the door. He didn't do repeats.

'Is there somewhere private where we can talk?' he asked and she lifted her chin.

'I'm working.'

Aaron folded his arms. 'You've been trying to get in touch with me, and now I'm here. What more do you want?'

She glared at him, clearly unwilling to relinquish her anger at his ignoring her messages for the last week. Then she nodded, her jaw set stubbornly. The woman was impossible, yet some contrary part of him admired her spirit. 'Fine.'

She turned to the other woman behind the counter, a twenty-something woman with purple hair and too many piercings, and said a few words. Then she stalked out of the shop, leaving Aaron, irritatingly, with no choice but to follow her.

'Well?' she said once they were out in the street, hands on her hips, pedestrians streaming by in an indifferent blur.

'I'm not about to conduct this conversation in the middle of a city street,' Aaron answered tautly. 'And I'd imagine you don't want to either.'

The fight seemed to leave her then and she sagged a little bit, looking, Aaron thought, suddenly very tired. 'No, I don't. But I have to get back to work.'

'As do I.' Every minute spent arguing with this woman was costing him in far too many ways. He simply wanted it dealt with and done. 'My limo is waiting. Let's at least conduct this conversation in the privacy of my car.'

With a shrug Zoe followed him to the sleek car idling by the kerb. Aaron jerked open the door and ushered her in, sliding in across from her. He pressed the intercom for the driver.

'Drive around the block a couple of times, please, Brian.'

'Very good, sir.'

He took a deep breath and stared hard at Zoe. 'Look, let's cut to the chase, Zoe. The baby isn't mine.'

She stared at him for at least thirty seconds, her gaze sweeping over him slowly, as if taking the measure of him—and finding it decidedly lacking. Not that he cared one iota about her opinion of him. Then she let out one short huff of laughter and looked away. 'You know, I had a feeling you'd go that route.'

'Of course I would,' Aaron snapped. 'I used protection.'

'Well, Super Stud, we're in the lucky two per-cent when that protection fails.'

'That's impossible.'

'Statistically, no. Two percent does not equal im-possible, genius.'

He closed his eyes for a second, willing himself not to lose his temper. He needed to stay in control of this conversation. 'Very unlikely, then.'

'I agree with you there.' She gave a rather grim smile. She didn't seem very pleased about this turn of events, Aaron realised. And she looked pale and drawn.

'So what do you want?' he asked, gazing at her levelly.

'From you? Nothing. If you want to deny being this baby's father, that's fine with me. I was only telling you as a courtesy anyway.' She met his gaze, grey eyes blazing, arms folded. Aaron felt a surge of alarm—as well as another tiny dart of admiration at her strength and courage.

'So you intend to keep this baby.'

Her gaze never wavered from his but he saw shadows in her eyes, like ripples in water. 'Yes.'

'I could demand a paternity test, you know.'

'Go right ahead. I looked into it, anyway. I can have one done at nine weeks.' Her mouth curved in a humourless smile. 'Then you'll finally be able to put your mind at ease.'

Her utter certainty shook him. Was she bluffing, or did she really believe this baby was his? *Could* it be his? The thought was terrifying. And surely—*surely*—impossible? 'How do you even know this baby is mine?' he asked in a low voice.

She pressed her lips together and glanced away. 'Contrary to the impression you've obviously formed of me, I don't sleep around. You're the only candidate, hot shot.'

He felt shock bolt through him as he acknowledged for the first time that she was actually pregnant with his baby. His *child.* He let out a long, slow breath, then lifted his grim gaze to hers. 'All right, then. How much do I have to pay you to have an abortion?'

Zoe blinked and sat back as if he'd struck her. She felt literally winded by his callous cruelty. The sweet passion she'd felt in his arms felt like a distant memory, absurd in light of their relationship—or lack of it—now.

'You really are a first-class jerk,' she said slowly. 'You couldn't pay me anything. I want to have this baby.'

His mouth tightened. 'Your life is hardly set up for a baby, Zoe.'

She bristled even as she recognised the stinging truth of his words. 'What do you know about my life?'

'You work in a coffee shop.'

'So?'

'You live in a fifth-floor walk-up in a bad neighbourhood.'

'It's a fine neighbourhood,' she snapped. 'And plenty of people who aren't millionaires living in mansions have babies.'

Aaron folded his arms. 'Why do you even want this baby?'

'Why don't you?' Zoe flung back. Aaron didn't answer, although she saw how he glanced away, as if he didn't want to answer the question.

'Well?' she demanded. 'I'm not asking you for anything, you know. I'll sign whatever piece of paper you want promising never to ask you for money or help, or even acknowledge you as the father. You don't have to be on the birth certificate. You're free, Aaron.' She flung her arms wide, the gesture mocking. 'Breathe a sigh of relief, because you don't have to have a single thing to do with this baby. I'd rather you didn't. But I'm keeping it.'

Aaron turned to gaze at her once more, his face utterly without expression. 'Twenty thousand dollars,' he said in a low voice.

Zoe's lips parted but no sound came out. 'Twenty thousand dollars,' she repeated tonelessly.

'Fifty thousand,' Aaron answered. 'More money than you've ever had in your life, I'm sure.'

'To have an abortion?' she clarified. He blinked, set his jaw even as his gaze flicked away once more. Even he wasn't willing to put it into such stark words. She stared at him for a long moment, wondering if he actually thought she might consider his offer for so much as a single second. 'You're serious,' she said, and with obvious effort he glanced at her again.

'I'm just trying to be reasonable.'

'You call this reasonable?'

Aaron's jaw tightened and for a second, no more, he looked almost panicked. 'I—I can't be a father.'

She let out a harsh, ragged laugh. 'Guess what? I'm not asking you to.'

'Zoe, think about it.'

She shook her head, nausea roiling inside her. It would serve him right if she were sick all over his precious car. 'Go to hell,' she finally said, her voice raw and, with the limo stopped at a traffic light, she got out.

Zoe walked down Christopher Street with her legs shaking. She felt physically ill, worse than any morning sickness she'd experienced so far. She thought of Aaron's unyielding expression as he'd offered her more money than she'd ever had before to get rid of their child.

Helplessly she turned aside and retched onto the sidewalk pavement. People hurried by, oblivious. Zoe didn't think she'd ever felt more wretched and alone. She'd dated plenty of commitment-phobic jerks in her time, but never someone as deliberately cold and cruel as Aaron Bryant. And he was her baby's father.

She straightened, took a deep breath and wiped her eyes. 'I hope, kid,' she muttered, 'that you favour my side of the family.'

By the time she returned to the café she thought she'd got herself more or less under control, although she obviously didn't fool Violet. The other woman raised her eyebrows as Zoe came in, handing a coffee to a customer.

'So that didn't go well,' she said as Zoe came behind the counter and reached for her apron. She just shrugged in response.

'Let me guess,' Violet said after they'd dealt with the latest trickle of customers and the café was mostly empty. 'That was the father.' Zoe nodded. Violet waited a few seconds. 'And?'

Another shrug. 'He's not thrilled.'

'We're talking serious understatement here, right?'

'Maybe.' Zoe took a breath and tried to banish the sight of Aaron's cold, autocratic expression as he'd offered her fifty thousand dollars. 'To be fair, it had to have been a huge shock.'

'To you, too.'

'Yes, but even so—' She stopped and shook her head. Why on earth was she defending Aaron to Violet, or to anyone? Why did she insist on believing the best about guys who didn't deserve it? And Aaron Bryant most definitely didn't deserve it. He was a cold-hearted bastard and she wouldn't give him one iota of her compassion or understanding.

And yet he was her baby's father. They were linked, fundamentally and forever, no matter what his actions. That counted for something, whether she wanted it to or not. She let out a long, slow breath and turned to Violet. 'Anyway, it doesn't matter. He's not going to be involved.'

Violet frowned. 'You're going to raise this kid on your own?'

Zoe heard the scepticism in her friend's voice and bit her lip. She thought of Aaron's scathing indictment: *your life is hardly set up for a baby.* No, it wasn't. She lived on a shoestring budget and her savings were virtually nil. Her apartment wasn't suitable for a baby, no matter what she'd told Aaron. She knew she could ask for help from her parents, or Millie and Chase, but the thought of their disappointment and censure—no matter if it was unspoken—made her cringe. Millie was the one who had got married, had a real job and lived an exemplary life. Zoe was the screw-up.

'Hey, Zo.' Violet put a hand on her shoulder. 'You know I'll help you, right? And so will lots of people, I'm sure. You can do this.'

Zoe blinked back sudden tears. Pregnancy hormones were clearly making her stupidly emotional. And while she appreciated Violet's offer, she wondered how much help a broke part-time college student could really give her…compared to how much she needed.

Two days later the morning sickness really hit and Zoe went from feeling a little nauseous to barely being able to get out of bed. She dragged herself to work and back again, and the rest of the time she curled up on her sofa and nibbled dry crackers, feeling utterly miserable. She thought about calling Millie, just to have someone to share this with. She knew she'd have to tell her sister as well as her parents some time, but for the moment she couldn't bring herself to admit her dire state of affairs. *I'm pregnant by your brother-in-law and he has no interest in this baby. He offered me fifty thousand dollars to get rid of it.* It was all just too, too awful.

And then one day it all changed. She went to the ladies' during a break at the café and there was blood in her underwear. Zoe stared at that single rusty streak in disbelief. Could she actually be having a miscarriage? After all she'd endured already, to have it end before it had even begun?

Tears pricked her eyes and her heart lurched. She realised in that moment just how much she wanted this child, despite the awful nausea and Aaron's horrible rejection.

'You look like you've seen a ghost,' Violet said when she came back into the café. 'What's going on?'

Numbly Zoe told her. 'You should see a doctor,' Violet said firmly.

'Can they even do anything at this stage?'

'I don't know, but do you want to take that chance? And it might give you some peace of mind.' She paused and added somberly, 'Either way.'

Duly Zoe picked an obstetrician from the internet—she had no friends who could recommend one—and made an appointment for that afternoon.

The OB, Dr Stephens, was a brisk grey-haired woman with a practical but friendly manner. 'Bleeding in early pregnancy can be perfectly normal,' she told her. 'But it also can indicate miscarriage. There's really no telling at this point. If you experience more bleeding, with any accompanying cramping, then you should come back.'

Zoe nodded dully. 'And is there anything I can do?'

'Nature generally takes its course at this point,' Dr Stephens told her gently. 'But of course staying off your feet and resting as much as possible couldn't hurt.'

Of course. Yet both of those were virtually impossible with her work.

As she walked back to her apartment, Zoe felt even worse. Going to the doctor hadn't reassured her; it had only made her aware of all the uncertainties, the impossibilities. She was only seven weeks' pregnant and already it was so unbearably hard…and lonely.

She sniffed, then took a deep breath. 'Pull yourself together,' she told herself as she unlocked the door to her building and kicked aside the drift of takeaway menus that always littered the floor. 'You can do this. You're strong. You've survived a lot.'

She thought of Tim and how devastated she'd felt then. Nothing, obviously, compared to what Millie had been going through at the same time, with the loss of her husband and daughter. Yet the aching loneliness of his betrayal and her inability to tell anyone reminded her of how she'd endured it; she'd got through, got stronger.

She could do this.

She headed up the five narrow flights of stairs to her tiny shoebox of an apartment; each step felt like a burden. How would she manage these stairs when she was nine months' pregnant? Or with a pram? And what would she do for childcare, for *money*?

Oh, God, what she was doing? She reached the top of the stairs and pressed the heels of her hands to her eyes, willing the tears to recede. She'd never cried so much in her life before.

'Zoe.'

She dropped her hands, shock icing through her, freezing her to the floor. Aaron stood in front of her door.

She looked terrible, Aaron thought. Her face was pale and gaunt, her hair stringy. And, even more alarmingly, she seemed near to tears, which he'd never seen before. He'd thought of her as strong, invincible, yet now she looked like she needed protecting. He felt a surge of concern, an unfamiliar emotion, and he took a step towards her.

'Are you all right?'

'Clearly not,' she answered tautly. 'But why do you care?' Without another word she pushed past him and unlocked the door to her apartment.

Aaron stood there, feeling weirdly and horribly uncertain. He hated doubt, hated how it crept inside him and poisoned everything he believed and knew. He hated feeling it now, and with it another rush of guilt for the way he'd acted. Of course Zoe didn't want to see or talk to him. He'd asked her—he'd offered to pay her—to get rid of their child. It had been an impulse born of desperation, but there was no going back from it. No forgetting, and perhaps no forgiving.

He'd realised that as soon as he'd seen the look of horror and shock on her face and knew he was its cause. He'd known what he'd done was unforgivable and he'd felt a sudden, cringing shame. Was he going to let his own fear control him that much? Was he going to be that weak, that cruel?

Now he stood in the doorway of Zoe's apartment and watched as she shrugged off her coat. She tossed it onto a chair and it slithered onto the floor. Her shoulders slumped.

'May I come in?'

'Why?' She straightened, tension radiating through her lithe body.

'I want to talk to you.'

'If you're going to try to strong arm me into—'

'I'm not.' Aaron cut her off. 'That was—that was a bad idea.'

She laughed dryly, the sound without humour. 'Quite a confession, coming from you.'

'May I come in?'

She shrugged wearily and turned to face him. 'Fine.'

Aaron stepped into the apartment, blinking in the gloom until Zoe switched on a light. The place was tiny, just one rectangle of a room with a bed, a sofa, a dresser and a tiny kitchen in the corner.

'I'm sure,' Zoe said dryly, 'it horrifies you to re-alise people live like this.'

He glanced at her, saw her eyes sparking with some of her old fire, a sardonic smile on her lips. '"Horrifies" might be too strong a word.'

'This is actually quite a nice apartment,' she informed him. 'According to some of my friends. At least I don't have to share.'

He stepped over some pyjamas that had been left on the floor and returned her coat to the chair. 'I can't imagine sharing a place this size.'

She watched him for a moment, her face with-out expression. 'What do you want, Aaron?' She spoke flatly, the fire gone.

'I want to discuss our child.'

'*My* child,' she corrected. 'I think you gave up any paternal rights when you offered me that money.'

Anger flared but he forced it down. 'I told you, that was a bad idea.'

'Oh, *well,* then,' she drawled. 'Never mind.'

All right, fine. Maybe he deserved this. He most assuredly did, but that didn't make accepting it any more pleasant. 'Look, I'm sorry, Zoe. I acted on impulse.'

'Some impulse.'

'I wasn't prepared to be a father.'

'I wasn't asking you to be a father,' she shot back. 'I was simply informing you that you'd unknowingly donated some DNA. You don't have to be involved in this baby's life. Frankly, I don't want you to be involved in this baby's life. I think he or she can do without a dad like you.'

Aaron blinked, her words wounding him far more than they should have. They *hurt*. 'Probably,' he said in a low voice, when he trusted himself to speak. 'I'll probably be a pretty lousy dad.' He certainly didn't have any good experience to draw from. He took a breath, let it out slowly. 'But I still want to be involved.'

Her jaw slackened and she stared at him with wide, dark eyes. *'What?'*

'I want to be involved, Zoe. I regret my earlier… suggestion. I told you, you caught me by surprise.'

'Remind me never to do that again, then.'

'I said,' Aaron said, hearing the edge enter his voice, 'I'm sorry.'

'And sometimes, Aaron, it's just not that easy. I can't forget. And I'm still not sure I want you involved.'

'I could—' He stopped, knowing a threat wasn't the right choice now.

'You could what?' she filled in. 'Take me to court? Sue for custody? With your money you'd probably win, too.'

Aaron said, his teeth gritted, 'I'd just like to have a civil conversation.'

Her shoulders sagged then and she sank onto the sofa, her head in her hands. He resisted the entirely ridiculous and inappropriate impulse to touch her, offer her some kind of comfort. He wouldn't even know how. 'Look, it's probably all irrelevant anyway.'

'Irrelevant? What do you mean?'

She glanced up at him, and with a jolt of alarm he saw the sheen of tears in her eyes. 'I had some bleeding,' she said dully. 'I might be having a miscarriage.'

Considering his earlier stance, Aaron knew he should be feeling relieved. But he didn't. He felt… alarmed. Worried. Maybe even sad.

'I'm sorry,' he said and Zoe's mouth twisted.

'Are you?'

'Yes, Zoe, I actually am. Can you just—please stop with the little barbed comments? For a little while, at least?'

She glanced down again. 'I'm sorry.'

'Have you been to the doctor?'

'Yes.'

'What did he say?'

'*She* said there wasn't much I could do right now. Nature will take its course.'

'That's not much of an answer.' Frustration fired through him. He'd never been the kind of person just to let things happen. From the moment he'd discovered Bryant Enterprises was virtually bankrupt, he'd been striving to bring it back from the brink. Even though several financial advisors had told him to just let it go, he'd refused. He'd worked endlessly to put his family's firm in the black and he'd work just as hard now. He didn't give up. He didn't *fail*.

'There must be something you can do,' he said, keeping his tone reasonable. 'Stay off your feet, rest.'

She shrugged. 'My life isn't like yours, you know. I can't just become a lady of leisure.'

He stared at her, thinking of her on her feet all day at the café, then tramping up five flights of stairs every night to this awful apartment. 'Actually,' he said slowly, the idea just starting to take shape, 'You could.'

Her brow wrinkled and she shook her head. 'What do you mean?'

Aaron, decisive now that a solution had presented itself, said, 'You could come and live with me.'

CHAPTER FOUR

ZOE STARED AT Aaron, his words, his offer, seeming to echo through the apartment.

'You're joking,' she finally said, and he shook his head, the movement brisk and decisive.

'I told you, I don't joke.'

She shook her head, everything in her rejecting what he'd suggested. 'Aaron, we barely know each other.'

'We're going to have a baby.'

She hated the thrill that coursed through her at his words, at that treacherous 'we'. 'A baby you don't want.' His dark brows came together in a frown but he said nothing and Zoe sighed. 'I'd drive you crazy.'

'Probably, but I work long hours.'

'So I'd drive myself crazy, wandering around your awful apartment all day long by myself.'

His incredulous gaze swept around her tiny studio. '*My* awful apartment?'

'All that cold chrome and steel. It's heartless.'

'So the reason you're objecting to this arrangement is my choice of decor?'

'No, of course not.' Zoe folded her arms, hating how he'd already got her on the defensive. Hating how a part of her, a terrible, treacherous part, actually already wanted to say yes. How stupid was that, when they obviously had no future? When staying with him would surely make her crazy, stubborn heart start thinking and hoping for things that were impossible? Things she shouldn't even really want? 'It's just not…practical.'

'This—' Aaron said, sweeping an arm around her apartment '—is not practical.'

Zoe bit her lip. 'It probably won't make a difference, anyway. I mean…what will be, will be.'

He shook his head. 'That's never been my philosophy in life.'

'No, I didn't think so.'

'Zoe.' He took a step towards her, his voice lowering in a way that made her want to shiver. 'Admittedly, there is a chance a bit of bed rest won't make any difference. But what if it did? Would you deny our baby that chance?'

Our baby. She bit her lip harder so it hurt. 'You're blackmailing me.'

'I'm just showing you reason.'

'It's not very fair.'

'Why don't you want to come live with me, have a few weeks' holiday?' He sounded exasperated now, as if he'd expected her to fall in with his plans far more quickly than this. 'You can have your own bedroom.'

'Given.'

'And we don't— We don't even have to talk to each other, if you don't want to.'

Zoe stilled. He sounded so oddly vulnerable then, so unlike the autocratic man she'd told herself she should despise. 'I think I could handle talking to you.' She relented, if only a little.

Aaron lifted an eyebrow. 'So what's the problem?'

So much for vulnerability. 'Why are you doing this? Offering this? Because it's about one hundred and eighty degrees from what you were suggesting a week ago.'

'I know that.' He pressed his lips together, colour slashing his cheekbones. 'I've had time to think, and I've…re-evaluated my position on the matter.'

'You've re-evaluated your position,' Zoe repeated. 'This isn't a board meeting, Aaron.'

'Will you come or not?'

She hesitated. Told herself this was a bad idea…
for her. But it was a good idea for the baby. It was
giving her baby—their baby—a chance. 'I could
just go to Millie and Chase's,' she said. 'Or my
parents'.'

'You could.'

But she didn't want to. Didn't want to admit to
them how desperate and alone she was. How she'd
messed up…again. And she knew, no matter what
she'd said to Aaron about emotional blackmail, she
couldn't deny her baby this chance. Working on
her feet all day and living in a fifth-floor walk-up
was not advisable with a threatened miscarriage.
She got that. She felt the fear, the guilt. She closed
her eyes, then opened them again. Nodded. 'Okay.
I'll come. For a few days, though. Maybe a week.'
She said this as much for herself, because Aaron
didn't respond to her addendum.

He slid his phone out of his pocket and issued a
few terse instructions. Then he glanced at her, his
gaze taking in the tiny apartment. 'You can pack
whatever you need. My car will be here in five
minutes.'

'Five *minutes*?'

A look of impatience crossed his features. 'I have
to get back to work. And the sooner this situation

is resolved, the better.' He turned away, scrolling through his messages as Zoe stood there, her mind whirling. *This situation.* That was what she was to him, she realised, what her—their—baby was. A situation. A problem he intended to solve as quickly and expediently as possible.

Swallowing, she turned and began to gather her things.

Sure enough, they were speeding uptown in his limo a matter of minutes later, Zoe's lone suitcase stowed in the back along with her house plant and one of her paintings. Aaron had eyed them askance and Zoe had said rather defiantly that she would not live in his morgue of an apartment without some colour.

'You can call the café where you work and give notice,' Aaron said, his gaze still on the little luminous screen of his phone.

'Give notice? It's only a leave of absence.'

He shrugged. 'Whatever. Either way I'll cover the rent on your apartment, so you don't have to worry about money.'

Zoe sat back against the seat, a new and different kind of nausea roiling through her. It might as well be her notice, she realised. Molly, the owner of the café, would have to hire a new barista while she was gone, and it wasn't as if Zoe was so valuable she'd dismiss that person when she was ready to return. Besides, when *would* she be ready to return? The future stretched in front of her, alarmingly unknown.

'I don't want to just sit around all day,' she said abruptly and Aaron glanced up from his phone.

'Even if that's best for the baby?'

'Enough with the emotional blackmail,' she snapped. 'I work afternoons as an art therapist, sitting down, very low-energy. I'm keeping that up.'

Aaron glanced at her in consideration before turning back to his phone. 'Fine. I'll arrange a car to drive you there and return you to my apartment.'

'Thank you,' she said stiffly, although she wasn't even sure what she was thanking him for. This *situation* felt uncomfortably like a prison sentence. She'd be let out for a few hours, but then swiftly returned to her cell.

Yet she'd agreed. She'd willingly put herself in Aaron's hands and, as the limo pulled up to the high rise she hadn't seen since that fateful night, she wondered why she had.

They didn't speak as they rode the lift up to the penthouse and the doors opened directly onto Aaron's apartment. Zoe walked through the cold, modern rooms and felt a prickling of discomfort lodge between her shoulder blades.

'This brings back memories,' she said lightly, because not saying it felt ridiculous, like refusing to acknowledge the elephant lumbering alongside them.

'New memories will take the place of those,' Aaron answered without emotion. 'Let me show you your bedroom.'

It was right across from his, and just as sumptuous, with a king-sized bed, a huge plasma-screen TV and an en suite bathroom with a sunken marble tub and walk-in shower. Zoe imagined soaking in that tub and felt some of her reservations start to crumble. It would be heavenly to relax for a little while, to have a break from all the worry and fear.

'Thank you,' she said, turning to Aaron. He stood in the doorway, dark and unsmiling. 'This really is very kind of you,' she continued awkwardly. 'I'm sorry if I haven't seemed gracious.'

'It's a difficult situation. And I haven't exactly handled myself with aplomb either.' He set her suitcase down. 'Why don't you unpack? I need to return to work but I should be back around dinner time. Order whatever you like. There are menus in the kitchen, and you can just charge it to my name.'

'Okay. Thanks.'

Then with a nod of farewell he was gone, and Zoe was left alone in the huge, barren apartment, her mind spinning as she wondered just what she'd got herself into.

She unpacked her few things as Aaron had suggested and then, because she was so tired and the tub looked so heavenly, she ran a huge, steaming bath and sank into the decadent bubbles with a blissful sigh.

Soaking in the tub she was reminded, suddenly and piercingly, of the night she'd spent with Aaron. After that first time on the rug he'd taken her to the bed, and then to the shower, soaped her everywhere, and then driven himself inside her while she had wrapped her legs around his waist…

Zoe closed her eyes as the memories assailed her and fresh, ridiculous desire coursed through her. She didn't want to remember the overwhelming passion of that night. It could only confuse what was between them now, which was essentially a business partnership. At least, that was how Aaron seemed determined to conduct it, and Zoe told herself it was sensible. She didn't want to get mired in feelings she had no business having for Aaron Bryant. No matter how great a lover he was, no matter how sweet his few and surprising moments of kindness, he was still, and always would be, an arrogant and autocratic jerk.

It felt weirdly disloyal to think that now, especially considering she was soaking in his bath tub as his guest for the foreseeable future. Yet Zoe knew she had to remind herself because, knowing her track record, if she didn't she just might start to fall in love with him—and that would be really, phenomenally stupid.

Aaron couldn't concentrate on his work, which was an irritating first. He was used to being able to focus completely on business; nothing else in his life even came a close second. Yet now, as he scanned the latest reports on the stock market in Asia, he found his mind drifting to Zoe. Wondering what she was doing. Was she watching TV? Taking a bath?

Instantly his body hardened as images flashed through his mind of Zoe in his tub with nothing but a few strategically placed bubbles popping slowly and revealing the soft, tantalising skin underneath—skin he'd touched, kissed, remembered the satiny feel of.

With effort he stopped that vivid montage from

reeling through his head. Unhelpful; he didn't want to think about Zoe as anything other than…what? His brain scrambled to compartmentalise her. He liked things tidy, in his control, yet nothing about this situation—about Zoe—felt that way. It had been messy and uncontrollable from the moment he'd met her, when she'd taken his phone and he'd responded by putting his hand up her skirt.

Sighing, Aaron raked a hand through his hair and tried to focus on the report in front of him. His mind had been spinning ever since that confrontation with Zoe in his limo. The look on her face when he'd made his cold-blooded offer. He cringed in shame at the memory, even as the aftershocks of surprise and even fear rippled through him. A baby. A father.

He'd never wanted to be a father. Never wanted to be that important to somebody—that critical. The opportunity to make a mistake, to *fail,* was too huge. And he knew first-hand the lasting damage a father could have on his son.

Yet over the last week he'd realised that, if Zoe was going to have this baby, if he was going to be a father whether he liked it or not, then he needed to be in that child's life. Being completely absent was surely one way to guarantee what he didn't want: to hurt an innocent child's life through his own faults and weaknesses.

Aaron glanced at the clock. It was nearly six, which was still several hours before he usually left the office, and then just to work more at home. Yet today he found himself closing his laptop, packing up his attaché case and heading outside into the still-warm September evening.

The apartment was quiet when he entered, alarmingly so. Had she left? Decided she didn't want to do this after all? And why did that thought alarm him so damn much?

Taking a deep breath, Aaron set down his case and shrugged off his jacket. He hated feeling this uncertain. This…worried.

'Hey.'

He turned to see Zoe coming out of the kitchen dressed in a T-shirt and yoga pants, her hair tousled and damp around her shoulders. She smiled, tucking her hair behind her ears. 'I had the most decadent afternoon. I probably should feel guilty.'

Decadent? His mind was leaping to possibilities and images he had no business thinking of. 'You came here to rest,' he said, intentionally noncommittal and even gruff. But Zoe didn't seem to notice and walked closer to him instead, so he caught the vanilla scent of her hair as she waggled her fingers in front of him.

'I spent two hours in the tub. My fingers still look like prunes.'

Aaron took a step away. 'I'm sure you'll recover.'

'I ordered Chinese for dinner. I know it's completely stereotypical for a pregnancy craving, but I really wanted some pork lo mein.'

'Your body must be craving MSG.'

She raised her eyebrows, a teasing smile curling her lush mouth. 'Wait a minute, did you actually make a joke?'

'A poor one, since the local Chinese place I order from doesn't even use MSG.' He took another step away from her, needing the distance. 'I think I'll go shower and change.' Wrong thing to say, he realised immediately. It made it sound as if they were going to have a cosy night in, eating Chinese food and watching TV. How ridiculous. How *impossible*.

This whole situation was incredibly awkward, Aaron thought as he escaped to the shower. He'd offered his apartment to Zoe on impulse, because when he saw a problem and he wanted to deal with it immediately. He hadn't considered how uncomfortably intimate it would be, sharing his living space, seeing her freshly showered and talking about Chinese food…

The whole thing was absurd. And messy. The sooner Zoe had a clean bill of health and could go back to her own life…

Except when would that be? he thought suddenly, his hands stilling in the process of scrubbing his hair. If the pregnancy continued to term, his life would always intersect with Zoe's in a most critical way. He needed to develop a plan. A strategy for the future. Except he had no idea what that could be.

First things first, he decided as he stepped out of the shower and wrapped a towel around his waist. He'd get through the next few weeks of uncertainty— Hell, first he had to get through this evening. Then he could think about what the long-term future for this unexpected family of theirs would be.

Zoe set out plates and glasses with no idea of what to expect. Would Aaron be joining her for dinner? Were they actually going to sit down and have a meal together, like some bizarre, instant happy family?

Despite her decadent afternoon, she felt exhausted. Maintaining a cheerfully insouciant facade—for she knew that was all it was—with Aaron was emotionally and physically draining. But it was also armour, a way to protect herself. To show him she wasn't bothered by this unusual living arrangement, that she wasn't remembering how he'd taken her right on that rug, with the lights of the city streaming over them. How for a moment, when he'd been inside her, she'd looked into his eyes and felt far more emotion than she ever wanted to feel… Even as she craved that connection once more.

Thankfully the intercom buzzed, calling a halt to that unhelpful line of thinking. By the time Aaron came out of his bedroom she was opening the steaming cartons of fragrant Chinese food, inhaling the blissful aroma of pork lo mein.

'You look like you've just died and gone to heaven.'

'It feels like it,' she admitted, and couldn't resist eating a forkful of noodles right from the carton. 'And normally I don't even like Chinese food.'

Aaron let out a rusty laugh. 'Those pregnancy hormones must be something.'

'I guess so.' She swallowed and smiled. 'What

do you like? We have the lo mein, General Tsao's chicken, moo shoo pork…'

The slight smile that had softened Aaron's features disappeared and he reached for a plate. 'I'll just have a bit of everything. And I'll eat in my study. I have work to do.'

Zoe felt the words like a rejection—and one she wasn't prepared to accept. 'You've been working all day,' she said mildly. 'And, not to sound like a nagging wife, but I'm not going to last if I have to stay in this morgue of an apartment by myself twenty-four-seven.'

Aaron frowned more in perplexity than irritation. 'What are you suggesting?'

'I think we can manage to eat dinner together,' Zoe said lightly. 'And, in any case, I want to talk to you about your decor.'

The look of patent disbelief on his face was both funny and satisfying, Zoe decided. 'My decor? Are you serious?'

'Completely.' She took her plate over to the sofa and sat down cross-legged, slurping another forkful of noodles before she resumed. 'I want to get some more things from my apartment.' His eyes widened and she held up one placatory hand.

'Don't freak, this isn't a permanent measure. But I like my things. They're *colourful*.'

'I wasn't freaking,' Aaron answered as he sat across from her, his own plate balanced in his lap.

'An eye flare is freaking for you,' Zoe tossed back. 'You are the master of control.'

'Now that's a compliment.'

'In your world, maybe.' She realised she was enjoying this banter, and the smile that twitched Aaron's lips made her heart sing. 'Anyway, back to the decor thing. I need to get some things from my apartment.'

'I can have someone take care of that.'

'I'd like to do it myself. God only knows what one of your minions would pick out.'

Aaron raised his eyebrows. 'My minions?'

'I need to go through it and see what I can bring back here. Not too much, just a few more paintings and things.'

She watched him process this, wondered how alarming it was for him to have her moving more of her stuff in. And, while it made sense, Zoe knew she was pushing just a little. She didn't really want to examine why.

'Fine,' Aaron said after a moment. 'I'll arrange a

car and driver. But I don't want you to exert yourself. No lifting things.'

'Yes, sir.' She smiled, his concern warming her heart—even if it shouldn't. He was just dealing with the situation. She was the one painting rainbows.

Three days later Zoe sat at a table in the East Village's community centre art-room, watching as Robert, a very self-contained boy of six, surveyed the materials she'd set out.

'What do you feel like doing today, Robert?' she asked gently. 'Crayons, markers, paints?' Robert had been coming to the centre for nearly a month, ever since his dad had walked out without any warning and hadn't been in touch since. He had barely spoken, had never touched the art materials, yet his mother kept bringing him in the hope that something would ease the pain he held so tightly inside.

'Maybe you could try a mandala today,' Zoe suggested, taking one of the simple designs of curved shapes that children often found soothing to colour. She placed it in front of him and Robert stared down at it silently for a few seconds before he finally selected a crayon and began to carefully colour in the shapes.

Zoe watched him, occasionally making some encouraging observation, when about halfway through Robert thrust his crayon away and reached for a black marker. She watched him in silence as he vehemently scribbled black marker all over the paper, obscuring the careful design. When the page was nearly all black, ripped in some parts from the force of his scribbling, he put the marker back in the jar and sat back, seemingly satisfied.

Zoe rested a hand on his shoulder. 'Sometimes we feel like that, don't we?' she said quietly. In truth she could relate to Robert's deliberate destruction. There was your life, all carefully set out in pleasing shapes, and something happened that cancelled it all out, scribbled over your careful planning.

Robert had felt like that when his father had upped and left. And Zoe felt like that now, pregnant and alone. Despite the friendliness of that first evening, Aaron seemed determined to avoid her whenever possible. Zoe had tried to draw him out, but the emotional effort exhausted her. She didn't want to have to try so hard. She wanted something to be easy, she acknowledged ruefully. But there was nothing easy about Aaron Bryant.

That morning she'd taken a few more things

from her apartment, pangs of both worry and regret assailing her as she had looked around the space she'd made her own, now empty and forlorn. A few weeks ago she'd had a home, a life, had been in control of her own destiny. Now she felt as if she were spinning in a void of unknowing and uncertainty.

Kind of like Robert felt now. She reached for a large piece of paper and the finger paints. 'Maybe,' she suggested, 'you'd like to do something messy?' The little boy was almost unbearably neat. 'Mess is okay here, you know. Everything washes off.'

He hesitated and she opened the paint pots, waited with a smile. A second later he carefully dipped one finger in the yellow paint and drew a single, cautious line on the paper, like a ray of sunlight. Zoe murmured something encouraging.

It was a start to unlocking the little boy's pain, to freeing those tightly held parts of himself. And she needed to start, too. She wasn't going to drift through the next few weeks like some desperate ghost. That had never been her style, even if men tended to bring out clinginess in her. She wouldn't be clingy with Aaron; she'd be in control. She'd claim her life back, even if it wasn't on the terms she really wanted.

She spent the rest of the afternoon arranging some of her things in Aaron's apartment, nerves battling with determination. She ordered Indian—she was methodically working through the take-aways—and set the table for two. Aaron made it home for dinner most evenings, and he almost seemed to enjoy the chatter she kept up resolutely, even if he sometimes seemed bewildered by the whole concept: dinner. Conversation. Company.

The lift doors swooshed open and Zoe turned. 'Hey there,' she said brightly and watched as Aaron's gaze moved around the apartment, taking in the plants lining the window sill and the two paintings she'd put on the walls, replacing some of the soulless modern atrocities he'd had hanging there. One canvas had been six feet of blank white with a single black splodge in the corner. Ridiculous.

'I see you've made yourself at home,' he said neutrally and Zoe gave him a teasing smile.

'I warned you, didn't I? At least this place has some colour.'

He stopped in front of an oil painting of a jar of lilacs on a kitchen table. The paint had been used liberally, creating, Zoe hoped, a messy yet welcoming feel.

'This is rather good, I suppose,' he said, sounding a bit grudging, and he turned to Zoe. 'Who's the artist?'

'Oh…no one famous.' She felt herself blush.

Aaron arched an eyebrow. 'Well, I didn't think it was Van Gogh. Is it a friend of yours?'

'Umm… It's mine, actually.' Both of the paintings were, and she suddenly realised how arrogant it might seem to hang her own art on his walls. She hadn't thought of that at the time; she just liked to be reminded of what she'd done, what she was capable of.

'I thought you were an art therapist, not an artist,' Aaron said, his brow furrowed, and Zoe shrugged.

'One's a profession, one's a hobby.'

'Did you ever want to be a professional artist?'

She shrugged. 'I don't really have what it takes. In any case, I like helping people.' She saw him frowning at her, as if she were a puzzle he didn't understand.

'I should work tonight,' he said abruptly, and Zoe's heart sank. Another night in front of the TV alone.

'Don't you get tired of working? It's practically all you do.'

'It's necessary.'

'Is it?' She kept her voice teasing. 'Will the company fall apart if you're not at the helm every second of the day, fingers twitching on your phone?'

Aaron's mouth tightened. 'It might,' he answered, and Zoe realised he was serious. Good grief, talk about a God complex.

'What happens when you get sick? Or go on vacation?'

'I don't.'

She shook her head. 'You're heading for a heart attack by the time you're forty.'

'Considering that's next year, I hope not.' He gave her the ghost of a smile. 'But thanks for the concern.' He took his plate, clearly ready to bury himself in his office. Again. Zoe took a breath and plunged.

'Aaron…how is a baby going to fit into your life, when it's like this?'

He stilled, slowly turned around. 'Surely we don't need to talk about that now?'

'Don't we? I know everything is still uncertain, but we need to think about the future. How it's going to work.'

'It will work,' he said tautly, and she shook her head.

'A baby isn't an item on your agenda, Aaron. It's a life commitment—'

'A week or so ago you didn't even want me involved,' he said shortly. 'Now you're talking about life commitments?'

Stung, she drew back. 'You're the one who said you wanted to be involved. I'm just trying to figure out how it will work.'

'It will work,' he repeated, and Zoe knew that was all he had: sheer determination and bullheaded arrogance.

'Why did you change your mind?' she blurted, because now she needed to know. 'Less than two weeks ago you would have paid me a large amount of money to have an abortion.'

'Are you ever going to let that go?'

'It's kind of a big one.'

'I know that.' He raked a hand through his hair and Zoe could see the lines of fatigue drawn from nose to mouth.

'What made you want this baby?' she asked quietly.

Aaron didn't answer for a long moment. Zoe couldn't tell a thing from his face, his eyes so dark and fathomless, the lines of his cheek and jaw harsh and strong in the dim light.

'I wouldn't have chosen this,' he said slowly. 'It's hardly an ideal situation for anyone. But I could see that you were determined to keep this baby, and if a child of mine was going to enter the world...' He paused, his gaze distant. 'Then I wanted to be involved.'

Zoe said nothing. She felt an almost crushing sense of disappointment, which was ridiculous. What had she expected? That Aaron had had some miraculous epiphany, realised he actually wanted to be a father, a family? No, of course not. Nothing in his behaviour in the few days had indicated anything but that he was making the best of a difficult situation.

'So,' she finally said. 'You'd still prefer me to have an abortion?'

'I didn't say that,' Aaron said, irritation edging his voice. 'If I did, I would have offered that instead of having you come live with me.'

'I don't understand you,' Zoe said quietly and Aaron shrugged.

'I'm not asking you to.'

The rebuff was brutal, even though it shouldn't even have surprised her. Of course he wasn't asking for such a thing. This domestic arrangement had nothing to do with their relationship or what little of it there was, Zoe reminded herself. That was clear from how rarely she'd seen Aaron since she'd come here, how much effort she'd had to put in to getting him to so much as sit with her for a meal.

'Maybe I should just go,' she said, and felt her throat thicken with humiliating tears. 'I haven't had any bleeding since that first time, and I can't lie around all day.'

'You're not lying around all day,' Aaron pointed out, an edge to his voice. 'You're working every afternoon.'

'You don't really want me here,' she forced herself to say. 'Do you?'

Another long, taut silence, and then Aaron finally spoke, the words dragged from him with obvious reluctance. 'Yes,' he said. 'I do.'

She tried for flippancy. 'You have a funny way of showing it.'

'I know I do.' He rubbed a hand over his face. 'Look, Zoe, I'm not good with emotions or feelings or even talking about…anything. I admit that. But I don't want you to go. I like having you here, knowing you're safe and cared for.' He paused and she saw a surprising vulnerability creep across his face, soften those stern features if only for a moment. 'Maybe the best solution is to make this… more permanent.'

'More permanent?' she repeated in disbelief. 'How?'

He took a breath, let it out. 'You stay here, with me, for the duration of your pregnancy.'

CHAPTER FIVE

ZOE DIDN'T SPEAK for a few seconds; she was still processing what Aaron had just said. *You stay here, with me, for the duration of your pregnancy.* Finally she said the first, the only, word she could.

'No.'

'Why not?'

'Because…' Her mind grasped at reasons he would understand, that she could admit to. *It's impossible. Dangerous. I might fall in love with you.* 'I just can't.'

'Can't?' he repeated. 'Or won't?'

'Both.'

'Why not?' He sounded so reasonable, so unruffled, and she felt as if she were falling apart. Aaron's suggestion, so calmly made, had rocked her to the core.

'Why should I?' she countered, knowing she sounded childish.

'It's not practical for you to live in some walk-up studio alone—climbing all those stairs.'

'I'll get a ground-floor apartment,' Zoe said numbly.

'Never mind that. What if something happened to you? Who would even know? As far as I can tell, you've lived a very independent, isolated existence.'

'I like being independent,' she snapped. She'd ignore the 'isolated' bit. 'Anyway, what about you? I think that's the pot calling the kettle black.'

'I don't deny it,' Aaron answered evenly. 'But I'm not pregnant.'

'Being pregnant doesn't mean being ill,' Zoe flung at him and his silence was eloquent. 'You don't want me here,' she said, daring him to deny it. *I like having you here.* She forced the memory of his reluctant confession away. Not helpful now, when she was trying to be strong.

'I just said I did,' Aaron answered, his voice taut.

'Just because you want to manage me.'

'Do the reasons really matter?' *Yes.* She swallowed, said nothing. Aaron sighed impatiently. 'Why are you so against it? It seems like an obvious and easy solution to me. You've already got your stuff here.' He swept one arm out towards her paintings, the wilting ficus plant. 'You still have your life. I've arranged a car for you to go to your little art sessions.'

'My little art sessions,' Zoe repeated numbly and Aaron sighed again.

'You know what I mean.'

'I know exactly what you mean. And that's the problem, Aaron. That's the prison.'

His mouth turned down and his eyes flashed darkly. 'What are you talking about?'

'You're the prison,' she said hopelessly, because she knew it sounded melodramatic and he wouldn't understand anyway.

He didn't. 'That's nonsense.'

'It's not. You have no idea what it's like living here with someone who barely wants to talk to you.'

'That's not true.'

'Who escapes at the first opportunity.'

'I do not.'

'And hides behind work.'

'I'm not *hiding*!' he thundered, the sound of his voice seeming to echo through the room and making Zoe fall silent. He let out an exasperated breath and raked a hand through his hair. 'Just what do you want from me, Zoe? Because I don't think it's something I have to give.'

'That's a great way to open a conversation.'

'I was trying to close it down,' Aaron snapped and Zoe shook her head.

'There's no point, is there?'

'Point to what?'

He looked so exasperated, so impatient, impervious and *blank*, and she knew he didn't get it at all. What was there even to get? What was she trying to prove here—that he didn't like her, wasn't interested in her other than as the mother of his unwanted child? *Obviously.*

'I don't know,' she whispered, all her fight and spunk gone in an instant, leaving only a weary despair. 'I don't know anything. I don't know why you want me here, what the future will look like, how you'll fit a baby into your life, never mind—' She stopped suddenly. *Never mind me.* Except he wasn't trying to fit her into his life—something else that was obvious.

Aaron didn't speak for a long moment. His irritation had gone, and he looked as weary as Zoe felt. 'Tell me what will make this work.'

She knew he meant it this time, knew this was how he operated. Life was simply a matter of function and success. But at least he was trying, at least he was waiting for her answer. She needed to try, too.

'I need more from you,' she said, and almost could have laughed at Aaron's involuntary recoil. 'I'm not asking for you to hold my hand or tuck me in bed.' She should not have mentioned bed. Or holding. Or even hands. Because everything made her think of how he'd felt on top of her, inside her. Touching her, loving her—except, stupid Zoe, because what had happened between them had had absolutely *nothing* to do with love.

'We need to figure out some kind of working relationship,' she clarified. 'If we're going to be involved in this together, as parents-to-be, never mind actual *parents*—'

'Let's cross that bridge when we come to it,' Aaron cut her off and Zoe nodded. One step at a time. One *minute* at a time.

'But even now, Aaron. I can't tiptoe around you. It'll drive me crazy.'

'I wasn't aware you were doing any tiptoeing,' he said dryly, and she let out a brief laugh of acknowledgement.

'All I'm asking for—and I know it might seem impossible, considering who we are—but can we try to get along? Be friends of a sort?'

He stared at her for a long moment, long enough for Zoe to feel like what she'd asked was impossible…at least for Aaron. And maybe it was for her, too. Contrary person that she was, half of her wanted to fall in love with him and the other half wanted to hate him. Typical.

'I hardly think it's impossible,' he said at last, and she couldn't tell a thing from his tone.

'That means,' Zoe explained, 'we have conversations. We eat dinner together—willingly. We ask about each other's day.'

'We paint each other's nails?'

She smothered a smile. 'That's the second joke you've made.'

'You must be having an influence on me.'

'Well, then?' she asked quietly. 'Could you do that? Could you try?'

Aaron let out a sigh. 'And if I do, will that be enough? Will you stay here willingly, for your pregnancy, and not complain or fight me every step of the way?'

'I'll try,' she said and his mouth quirked in a small smile, lightening his features and making her realise how rarely he smiled. How much she wanted him to.

'Then we'll both try,' he said, and held out his hand. 'Deal?'

She took his hand and let it enfold hers, felt the warmth and strength of it all the way through her. 'Deal,' she answered back.

How the hell was this supposed to work? Aaron stared moodily at the screen of his laptop as he mentally reviewed last night's conversation with Zoe. So he was just supposed to ask about her day? Eat at the same time? Instinctively Aaron knew Zoe wanted more than that. She wanted…what? A companion? A friend?

And Aaron didn't know how to be a friend. He didn't *have* any friends. He had employees, colleagues, acquaintances, siblings. None of them were friends. He'd been too private, too focused on work, too afraid of showing his weaknesses.

So how was he supposed to be a friend to Zoe?

He exhaled in an impatient sigh, resenting everything about this situation. Yet what could he have done instead? Installed Zoe in a separate apartment, he supposed, with staff. Instinctively he recoiled against such an idea, knowing she would hate it. He didn't like it much, either. She made him anxious, angry and impatient, yet he'd meant what he said. He liked having her around. He liked the sound of her laugh, the bright art on the walls, the feeling that he wasn't alone.

Good Lord. What was happening to him? And how did he make it stop?

He was still pondering the whole problem in his car on the way back to the apartment, the windows open to the warm, early-autumn air. His unseeing gaze suddenly focused on a shop sign and he pressed the button for the intercom.

'Stop the car, please.'

Fifteen minutes later he was entering the penthouse, bag in hand. Zoe lay on the sofa, a magazine sliding from her loosened fingers, clearly asleep.

He watched her for a moment, saw how her dark lashes feathered her cheeks, her lush lips parted softly on a sigh. Her hair was tousled and spread across the sofa pillows, dark and lustrous. She looked like something out of a fairy tale, he thought suddenly, like a princess who would be wakened by a kiss.

And he wanted to be the prince that kissed her.

Not that he would. He didn't even move. Getting physically involved with Zoe at this point was dangerous. Physically dangerous, considering the state of her pregnancy, and emotionally dangerous, as well. Not for him—hell, he barely had emotions. But for her… He didn't want to complicate their situation any more than necessary. Even if right now it seemed like the most appealing thing to do.

Zoe's eyes fluttered open then and she blinked sleepily. 'I must have fallen asleep.'

Aaron felt a smile tug at this mouth, his heart inexplicably lightening. 'Clearly.'

'Sorry.'

'That's what you're here for. To rest.'

'Yes, but…' She struggled up to a seated position. 'I had dinner warming. I ordered Thai this time. I felt like sticky rice.'

'All these cravings.'

'I know. Crazy.'

He walked to the kitchen and peered in the oven where several foil cartons were warming. 'I'll dish it out,' he offered and was rewarded with a cautious smile.

Maybe this wouldn't be so bad, he thought as he ladled rice and vegetables onto two plates. Maybe Zoe just wanted a little conversation, a little company. Maybe he could handle that.

He came back with the plates and handed one to Zoe. She took it with a murmured thanks, her feet tucked up under her, her cheeks flushed. She looked pretty, he thought. Rosy and even blooming. Wasn't that what you said about pregnant women? Like flowers.

'What did you get up to today?' he asked after a few minutes of silence. He was conscious of how awkward he felt, making small talk. He didn't do chit-chat. He gave orders, he listened to reports, he got things done. He shifted in his seat and ate another forkful of rice.

'Not much,' Zoe answered with a sigh. 'I went for a short walk, I read a book, I planned my lesson for tomorrow and then I fell asleep.'

'You're bored,' Aaron said, and he could hardly blame her.

'Out of my mind.' She smiled ruefully. 'I like being busy. I know it might not be reasonable to work on my feet at the café all day, but I need something more to do.'

As always Aaron went for solutions. 'Could you take on more hours with the art therapy?'

She shook her head. 'There's so little funding for it already. I'd love to do it full-time, but budgets are being slashed left and right.'

'What is art therapy, exactly?'

Her eyes glinted mischievously. 'My little art

sessions? Technically it's the therapeutic use of art-making.'

'Which is?'

'Using art as a form of communication and healing for a variety of situations. I work with children who have usually experienced some kind of difficulty—whether it's a death, divorce or some trauma in their family.'

'And they just…draw pictures?'

'I know it probably sounds like a waste of time to you.'

'Don't put words in my mouth,' Aaron answered, although frankly it did. How could scribbling on some paper be of any help to anyone, child or adult?

'Sometimes,' Zoe said quietly, 'it's easier to express yourself through art than through words, especially for a child.'

'I suppose,' he allowed, and she gave him a small smile, as if she knew how sceptical he was. She probably did. 'You should try it. You seem to have enough trouble expressing your emotions.'

He tensed, then strove to stay light. 'Are you actually analysing me?'

'I wouldn't dare.' She spoke as lightly as he had, but he knew she was serious and he prickled with discomfort. 'Why is it so hard for you, Aaron? Why did you tell me you weren't good at speaking about feelings—or anything?' She cocked her head, sympathy in her studious gaze. 'Were you not encouraged to do so as a child?'

'Is that what the textbooks say?'

She shrugged. 'It's usually a fairly good guess.'

He really didn't want to talk about himself. He never did. Yet he also knew he'd hurt Zoe if he tried to brush her off now; even that realisation surprised him. Since when did he consider anyone's feelings at all? 'I guess I wasn't,' he said after a moment, as if it were no matter. And really, it wasn't. 'We weren't ever a close family.'

'Why not?'

'I don't really know. My father was busy—elsewhere.' With his mistresses, but Aaron didn't want to reveal that much.

'And your mother?'

'Stop the interrogation, Zoe.' He heard an edge to his voice. 'I'm not one of your patients.'

Her eyes darkened but she smiled in rueful acknowledgement. 'Sorry. Habit, I guess.'

'I don't need therapy,' Aaron said, trying to make a joke of it even though he still felt on edge. 'And certainly not art therapy. I can't even draw stick figures.'

'That doesn't matter.' She shook her head and smiled, although he suspected it took some effort. 'I suppose I'll never make a convert of you.'

'Do you want to?'

'It would be nice if you respected what I did,' she answered, eyebrows raised, and Aaron grimaced.

'I'm afraid I'm too much of a literalist. I like firm results—tangible, quantifiable proof.'

'Life doesn't always work that way.'

He shook his head. 'Mine does.'

She stared at him, her head cocked to one side, her gaze sweeping slowly, thoughtfully over him in a way Aaron didn't like. 'And you don't feel like you're missing out on something, living like that?'

'No, I don't. I get results. Quantifiable success.'

'And healing isn't quantifiable,' Zoe surmised. 'Is it? Or happiness?'

'No, they aren't.'

She stared at him again and he felt everything inside him tense, resisting the very nature of this conversation, this *intimacy*.

'Are you happy, Aaron?'

Damn it, he did not want her to ask questions like that. He most certainly didn't want to answer them. 'What's happy?' he said, dismissive, gruff, and she smiled wryly.

'That's not an answer.'

He wasn't going to give her one. 'Are *you* happy?' he threw back, and she drew her knees to her chest, her hair brushing the tops of them, her eyes dark and soft.

'I don't know. Everything is so uncertain now. But, in general, yes. I think I've been happy. I've lived my life happily…for the most part.'

He had the strangest sensation that she was holding something back…just as he was. And he felt a stirring of uneasy guilt that she wasn't happy now, and it was his fault.

'Let me get dessert,' he said, mostly because he'd had enough of this conversation.

'Dessert?'

'I bought something. I figured you were going for the typical pregnancy cravings, so…' Quickly he went to the freezer where he'd put the bag from earlier and withdrew a pint of chocolate-chip ice cream. 'Have you had a craving for this?'

The look on her face was almost comical, Aaron thought. She looked torn, caught between regret and a smile, and he knew immediately this wasn't something she wanted.

'Don't tell me I'll have to eat this all by myself,' he said, and she gave in to the smile, whimsical and bittersweet as it was.

'I'm afraid I'm lactose intolerant. But it was a lovely thought.'

'Ah.' Lactose intolerant; right. He put the ice cream back in the freezer. 'So maybe a nice sorbet?' he suggested. He felt like a fool and a failure, which he knew was ridiculous. It was just ice-cream—and yet he'd tried. And it hadn't worked. Failure.

'Sorbet would be perfect,' Zoe said quietly, and then she was there behind him, one hand resting lightly on his shoulder. 'Thank you, Aaron,' she said softly, and for some ridiculous reason his throat tightened. He didn't answer.

It wasn't much, Zoe knew, and yet it touched her all too deeply. The hesitant confidences, the thoughtful touches... He was trying. Not very well, admittedly, but his attempts at engaging her emotionally made Zoe's heart soften and yearn. She could fall in love with this man, more than any of the men she'd convinced herself she cared for. She had a horrible feeling this could be the real deal.

And she didn't want it. She couldn't. Aaron might be trying, but that was all it was. Paltry attempts that she wanted to make into so much more. In the end the result would be the same: he'd break her heart. He'd crush it and he wouldn't care—or perhaps even notice.

A few days after Aaron's ice cream attempt, he came home a bit early, surprising her, and she tried to ignore the little bolt of pleasure she felt at simply seeing him walk through the door, his suit jacket hooked over one finger.

'You're home a bit early.'

'I have an invitation to a new museum opening in SoHo tomorrow night,' Aaron said. 'And I wondered if you wanted to come.'

'Oh.' She felt an unexpected burst of pleasure at the thought of a proper outing—almost a date. 'I'd love to.' She bit her lip, frowning. 'Is it fancy? I don't really have…'

'You can get something tomorrow. I'll leave you my credit card.'

Zoe arched an eyebrow, deliberately teasing him. 'You're not worried I'll go on a bender and max out your card?'

'I'm protected against such possibilities,' Aaron

answered, without even a shred of humour. Zoe suppressed a sigh. Just when she thought they were getting somewhere—reaching some kind of understanding, some kind of sympathy—she felt as if she'd fallen backwards on her behind. Aaron had only offered her his credit card knowing that if she ran off with it he'd be covered. Of course.

'Well, that's a relief,' she said lightly.

'Of course, if you'd rather not shop I can have my assistant buy you something,' Aaron offered. He'd loosened his tie and stood at the kitchen counter, drinking a beer. If someone could look in the window and see this scene, Zoe thought suddenly, it would seem so amazingly, achingly normal. A man and a woman chatting about their day, sharing the occasional smile or even a laugh.

Too bad the reality was so different—so much *less.* And she wanted more. Absurd, hopeless, but she could not keep herself from feeling it, craving it.

'Why don't you have your assistant pick something, then?' she said, and with effort kept her voice casual. 'I don't really like shopping.' That much was true, but she also needed to keep some kind of distance. Picking out a dress herself, knowing she'd care too much and want to please Aaron, was dangerous. If she acted like she didn't care what she wore, then maybe she wouldn't. Maybe her foolish, contrary heart would stop insisting it cared about Aaron when her head told her what an idiotic thing that would be to do.

'Fine,' he answered with a shrug. 'I'll have her pick it out and deliver it. The opening is at eight.'

When the box came the next afternoon, clearly from an exclusive and expensive boutique, Zoe couldn't keep a tremor of anticipation from going through her. She might not particularly enjoy shopping, but what woman didn't enjoy receiving new clothes? Even if they had been picked out by an indifferent secretary.

The dress wasn't indifferent, though. The dress, Zoe saw as she lifted it from the folds of tissue paper with a hushed breath, was utterly gorgeous. It was made of a silvery-grey silk that shimmered in the light, with a halter neck and a fitted bodice, before flaring out gently around the ankles.

She stripped off her jeans and T-shirt and slid the dress on, twirled around it and felt like a princess.

What would Aaron think?

Not important, she told herself. Not important

at all. She was just going to enjoy herself tonight, enjoy being out and about and feeling pretty rather than something close to what the cat dragged in. And she wouldn't think about Aaron at all.

She slid the dress on a hanger and, with a smile still lingering on her lips, headed for the bath.

Several hours later she was dressed and ready. And Aaron hadn't even returned. He'd texted to say he'd be back to pick her up at a quarter to eight, but it was almost the hour and she'd had no word from him.

Sighing, Zoe stared at her reflection. At least she looked better than she had in days. She'd put her hair up in a chignon and even put on a little make-up: eye-liner to make her eyes look bigger and darker and some light blusher and lipstick.

In the box underneath the dress she'd found a pair of diamanté-encrusted stilettos, perfect to go with the dress, and amazingly in her size. She gave a twirl in front of the mirror just as she heard the lift doors ping open and Aaron come into the apartment.

Taking a deep breath, she stepped out into the hallway.

His gaze narrowed in on her right away, but he didn't say anything. Zoe held her breath, waiting—

for what? A compliment? A single word of praise? Surely even Aaron could manage that much.

He tugged at his tie and gave one brusque nod. 'It fits.'

It fits? That was all? Disappointment made Zoe's throat tighten and she swallowed, made herself smile. 'Yes, it does. Your assistant must have known my size.'

Aaron didn't answer for a moment, his long, lean fingers working the silken knot of his tie. 'My assistant didn't buy it,' he finally said, sounding both gruff and reluctant.

Zoe blinked. 'She didn't?'

'No.' The knot unravelled and he slid his tie off, causing Zoe's gaze to be hopelessly drawn to the lean, brown column of his throat, the pulse she could just see flickering there as he undid the top buttons of his shirt.

'Who did, then?'

'I did,' Aaron admitted. 'I picked it out myself.'

Pleasure flooded through her in a warm rush and a silly smile spread over her face. 'You did? Why?'

'Because,' he answered, starting towards his bedroom, 'I didn't want the gossip flying, as it would if my assistant started shopping for a woman's dress. It's not my usual behaviour, and I hardly want to explain our situation just yet.'

Disappointment replaced that rush of pleasure. Of course he had a reason like that. Had she actually hoped, actually *thought* for a moment that he'd picked the dress out himself because he wanted to? What kind of fantasy land was she living in?

'Very astute of you,' she called to him, for he'd disappeared into his bedroom. 'But when do you plan on coming clean with our arrangement?' Whatever their *arrangement* actually was.

'When things are a bit more final,' Aaron answered back flatly. 'I'm just going to change. The limo's waiting downstairs.'

Zoe paced the living room while he dressed. All her anticipation about the evening, her pleasure in the dress and the shoes, seemed to have leaked right out of her, leaving her flat. And not just flat, but anxious—for what on earth did Aaron mean, when things were a bit more *final*? The decisions she'd made in moving in here felt all too final. What more was Aaron thinking of? She didn't even want to ask. She didn't want to know.

And, instead of the excitement and fragile happiness she'd been feeling at the prospect of an evening with Aaron, all she felt now was disappointment and an inexplicable, nauseating dread.

CHAPTER SIX

AARON CHANGED INTO his tuxedo with jerky movements, his body still irritatingly affected by the sight of Zoe in that dress. He'd known it was right for her as soon as he'd seen it in a shop window, imagining how the silvery fabric would bring out the shimmer in her eyes.

He'd felt a fool blundering into that shop. The sales assistant had positively cooed over him, imagining he was buying a dress for someone special.

And then when he'd actually seen Zoe in it, seen how the colour made her eyes sparkle with the brilliance of diamonds; how the silky material clung to her slender curves, the top barely covering the breasts that looked even more full and more lush than when he'd touched them, kissed them and held them in his hands…

He cursed aloud. The last thing he needed was to go into this evening in a constant and painful state of arousal. Yet he couldn't deny that since he'd been spending more time with Zoe that had been his sad state of affairs. Just sitting next to her on the sofa, or watching her slurp her ridiculous lo mein noodles, or stretch so her worn T-shirt outlined her breasts all too clearly…

Aaron cursed again.

Over the last week his mind had spun in crazy circles, thoughts darting like a rat in a maze, looking for solutions. Always looking for solutions. Ever since that first lightning strike of guilt that had felled him after he'd offered her money, he'd been trying to figure out how this could work, what he should do. He always wanted, needed something to do—a plan, an answer. And unfortunately, in this case, he didn't have one. Yet.

Having Zoe live with him had felt like the right decision; he wanted her safe, under his watch, in his control. And, damn it, yes, he did like having her here, even if she didn't believe him and he couldn't quite believe it himself.

But what about the future? When the baby was born? They'd be a family, of sorts. A *family*. The idea was alien, impossible. His own fractured family, with parents long dead and brothers he barely talked to, was hardly an example he wanted to follow. He didn't want to be the kind of dad who breezed in and out of his child's life, gone more often than not.

Yet he didn't know what kind of father he could be, what kind of man he could be. What kind of husband.

He'd been moving carefully, reluctantly, yet with a surprising surge of anticipation towards what seemed like the obvious decision, the most permanent arrangement for him and Zoe. It had come to him in stages: first asking Zoe to stay for a few weeks, then for her entire pregnancy. And now...?

His mouth curved grimly. It wasn't ideal, of course, even if it had some rather obvious and salient benefits. But it was the solution that had presented itself, that seemed the most reasonable—and yet outrageous. Impossible, even.

By the time he emerged from the bedroom Zoe was looking a bit pale and strained, the obvious pleasure which had lit her eyes damped down completely—his effect on her, no doubt. He should have said something else, something about how beautiful she'd looked, yet the words had stuck in his throat, sharp and painful. Grimly Aaron jerked his head towards the door.

'Let's go. The car's waiting.'

'I know, you said that already,' she answered back tartly, and Aaron didn't respond. Bickering like an old couple already, he thought sourly, without so much as a shred of humour.

Neither of them spoke in the limo on the way down to SoHo. Zoe stared determinedly out of the window, and the passing streetlights highlighted the sweep of her cheek, the angle of her jaw. Aaron watched her out of the corner of his eye—was conscious of every breath she drew, the way her breasts rose and fell, the tiny sigh of exhalation. He turned away and stared out the other window.

'So what kind of art are we going to go and see?' she finally asked, after the tense silence had gone on for several minutes.

'I don't know. Something modern.'

'Why are you going, then?' Zoe asked. She sounded petulant, even childish. This evening was going downhill fast.

'Several of my clients will be there.'

'Clients? What is it you do, exactly?'

'I'm the CEO of Bryant Enterprises.'

'I know that. But what does that mean?'

It means I live on a knife-edge; I wake up at night in a cold sweat; I devote my entire life to a job I never really wanted. The sudden virulence of his thoughts shocked him. Swallowing, he turned back to the window. 'I manage the company's assets, which are varied. But my main personal responsibility is our hedge fund.'

'That's what Millie does—hedge funds. Although I'm not even sure what they are.'

'Essentially an investment fund with a wider range of trading activities than other funds.'

'Still not sure what you're talking about,' Zoe said airily, and Aaron almost smiled. He actually liked that she didn't get it. He didn't really want to explain it, or even talk about it.

'Hedge-fund managers usually invest some of their own money,' he told her. 'And the funds are not sold to the public or retail investors.'

'So you're managing your own money, as well as someone else's?'

'Essentially.'

She turned to face him, her expression strangely serious and intent in the darkness of the car. 'Do you like it?' she asked. 'Do you enjoy what you do?'

Aaron stared back at her, words lodging in his throat, choking him. 'I make money,' he finally said.

'So?'

'It's what I do,' he answered, and made his tone dismissive, even curt. 'It's what I've always done, what my family has always done.' There were no other choices.

Zoe felt her spirits lift as soon as they entered the gallery. It was all soaring space and clean angles, huge, messy canvases hanging on the otherwise stark walls. Women in elegant dresses and men in tuxedoes circulated the space amidst black-tied waiters with trays of champagne and fussy-looking hors d'oeuvres.

'I know you're not keen on modern art,' Aaron murmured as they came through the door, and Zoe arched an eyebrow.

'Who said I didn't like modern art?'

'You did say my apartment was awful,' Aaron reminded her. 'And it's rather modern.'

'True, but there are different kinds of modern. My paintings are modern, in their own way. These—' she gestured to the bright canvases on the walls '—are colourful, lively. I like them,' she stated firmly and Aaron gave the nearest painting his consideration.

'I'm not sure what it's supposed to be.'

Zoe studied it, as well. 'From a distance it looks

like some kind of festival,' she said slowly. She couldn't point to any distinct figures or shapes, yet she got the sense of it—of people with arms outstretched or raised, of firelight and dancing, of joy and celebration.

Aaron nodded slowly. 'Yes…I suppose,' he said, and Zoe laughed at how dubious he sounded.

'Not a fan?' she teased. 'And with all that modern art in your apartment!'

'I never said I liked it. I certainly didn't choose it.'

'Why have it if you don't like it?'

He shrugged. 'An interior decorator chose it all, for effect and re-sale value. I spend very little time there as it is.'

'And yet I spend a lot of time there,' Zoe replied tartly. 'Maybe I should redecorate.' She saw the expression on Aaron's face freeze and she rolled her eyes. 'Chill, Aaron. I was joking. I'll stick with my few paintings and my plant. That's enough for you, clearly.'

'You can redecorate if you want,' he said stiffly. 'Since you'll be living there for at least seven months.'

At least. Because what happened after the baby

was born? Zoe pushed the thought away. 'I want to study the painting,' she said, and moved closer.

Funnily enough, the closer she got to the painting the less of a sense of it she had. The festive feeling melted into blobs and streaks of oil paint, nothing more. After inspecting a few more paintings in the gallery, she realised this was the artist's intended effect: the paintings were meant to be viewed from a distance, rather than up close.

Kind of like her and Aaron. From a distance, they looked okay. Like a couple. She'd seen a few women shoot her speculative and even envious looks, and part of her had wanted to laugh, even while another part of couldn't help but preen. *Yes, I'm with him, the most handsome and enigmatic man in the room.*

Except she wasn't with him, not really. Not at all.

She watched him covertly from across the room, talking to a few of his clients. He looked intent and serious and still so unbearably attractive, with his dark hair and eyes, his stern mouth, his broad shoulders. He was devastating in a tuxedo.

As if he sensed her looking at him, he glanced up and his steely gaze locked with hers for a moment, his expression utterly unreadable, and then he looked away. Zoe felt herself deflate. What had she been hoping for—a smile? A wink? Neither, unfortunately, were Aaron's style, and yet her stupid heart kept insisting on hoping.

By half past ten her feet were killing her—as gorgeous as the stilettos were, comfort was clearly not their concern—and she was nearly swaying with exhaustion.

Aaron approached her, one hand sliding firmly under her elbow. 'You look like you're about to fall over.'

'I feel like it too,' Zoe admitted with a small smile that ended on a tired sigh.

'Let me take you home.'

Home. She thought of that stark penthouse apartment where she'd already spent so many lonely days and nights. Was that home now? Would it ever be home?

Still, it was rather nice to have Aaron acting a little protective of her as he guided her from the gallery to his waiting car.

'How does your driver never get a parking ticket?' she asked as she slid inside. 'He's always double-parked.'

'He's very good,' Aaron answered. 'And he's not double-parked for long—I text him right before I need him to arrive.'

'A good use for your phone,' she said rather sleepily, for in the warm interior of the car, the leather so soft and luxurious, she felt as if she could almost fall right asleep.

'Come here,' Aaron said almost roughly, and he put his arm around her shoulders, pulling her to him. She nestled against him instinctively, her head on his shoulder, her body snuggled against his muscular side. It felt so good to be held; to breathe in the warm, musky male scent of him; to feel the solid strength of his arm around her, drawing her close, protecting and even cherishing her.

'Thank you,' she murmured, her eyes drifting closed. 'For taking me to the gallery. I enjoyed it.'

'Did you?' Aaron sounded as gruff as always, but underneath Zoe thought she heard a thread of amusement, maybe even tenderness. Or was she just being fanciful—again? Probably. 'The last twenty minutes you looked like you were in agony.'

'These shoes hurt,' she admitted and wiggled them off, stretching her toes with a sigh of bliss.

'Ah. Sorry about that.'

'Did you pick the shoes out too?'

'The shop assistant suggested them to me.'

'Well, I love them, no matter how much they pinch.'

'I didn't mean to make your feet hurt.' She felt Aaron's hand slide down her calf and then his strong fingers were kneading the aching muscles of her feet and Zoe couldn't keep from letting out a groan of sheer pleasure. Aaron chuckled softly. 'Feels good?'

'Heaven.' She nestled closer and neither of them spoke as Aaron massaged her feet. Zoe fell into a doze, happier than she'd been in a long while.

She didn't know how long it had been when Aaron was gently nudging her awake. 'We're here,' he said quietly. 'Can you make it upstairs?'

'Yes, of course.' She straightened, embarrassed now at how she'd been cuddling into him. 'I can hardly have you carry me into your building.'

'I could,' he said, and she found herself smiling.

'I'm sure you're strong enough. But, if you thought having your assistant buy a dress would bring on the gossip, sweeping me into your building Rhett Butler style would be much worse.'

'That doesn't matter,' he said abruptly and she wished she hadn't said anything—wished she'd let that surprising tenderness they'd found inside the limo stretch on. Now she just slipped her feet into the pinching heels.

The crisp night air was enough to wake her up

completely, and by the time they reached the lift Zoe was conscious of something palpable between them, something confused and yet electric, caught between the intimacy of their moments in the car and the tension that always seemed to spring up between them.

She was achingly aware too of the last time she'd been in a formal dress and Aaron had worn formal clothes. They'd rode the lift up in silence just like they were doing now, and she'd walked into his apartment and stared out at the night sky while he kissed her neck…

Was he remembering that night? Was he feeling it, wanting it like she was? Or was that just her hopeless fantasy?

She cleared her throat, the sound as loud as a gunshot in the confined space of the lift. The doors swooshed open and Zoe stepped into the penthouse, wanting to escape the confines of the lift and the expectations and memories that left her breathless and desperate with need.

The stiletto heel of her shoe caught in the gap between the lift and the floor, and she pitched forward with a sudden, indrawn gasp. Then Aaron's arms were around her, righting her, hauling her to safety against his chest.

She stared up at him, dazed, even more breathless than before, and he looked back down at her without any expression at all lighting his dark eyes.

'That was a close one,' he said, and he didn't let her go.

Zoe could feel one hand on her bare shoulder, the other seeming to burn right through the thin silk of the dress, on the small of her back. She felt the press of his body against hers, the strength of his thigh and chest, and then, amazingly—yes, wonderfully—the insistent press of his arousal.

Her lips parted and her breath came out in a soft, expectant rush; still she didn't move and neither did he. She felt his hand pressing into her back, urging her forward, and as her hips bumped against him his awareness flared white-hot, consuming her.

She knew they couldn't have sex. She didn't want to endanger her pregnancy, and she knew Aaron wouldn't take that risk either. Yet the need between them was palpable, overwhelming. Aaron's hand slid from her shoulder along her bare arm, the touch of his fingers seeming to dust her with sparks. He dipped his head lower and Zoe's own fell back, her lips parted and waiting for his kiss, every nerve inside her buzzing and humming.

'Zoe…' Her name was the softest of sighs and she felt his thumb brush her lower lip. She let out a tiny sound of want, halfway between a mewl and a moan.

With a shuddering breath, Aaron stepped away. 'You should go to bed.'

She felt as if he'd doused her with ice-water but somehow Zoe managed to nod, disappointment, a little relief and a terrible, aching unfulfillment all warring within her. 'Yes, I should.'

Aaron turned away, raking his hands through his hair before yanking off his tie. Zoe watched him, knowing he had to be as sexually frustrated as she was. She didn't want the evening to end here. She didn't want to go to bed alone. She swallowed, her throat dry, her heart beating hard.

'Aaron…'

'What?' His back was still to her, every taut line of his beautiful body radiating tension.

She shouldn't want this. Definitely shouldn't ask for it. Yet something—some great, deep need that had opened up inside her—compelled her to continue, to say aloud what she so desperately craved. 'Would you…sleep with me tonight? I mean just sleep. In the same bed.'

Aaron stilled, said nothing. Zoe felt herself

flush, her insides seeming to hollow out. Then he slowly turned around; in the moonlit darkness she couldn't make out his expression. Not that she would have been able to, anyway.

'What for?'

What for? Did she really have to spell it out? Apparently. 'For company. And closeness. And because…' She swallowed, her voice dropping to a ragged whisper. 'I'm lonely.'

He stared at her for a long moment. 'I always sleep alone.'

'You slept with me that night—that other night.' She licked her lips, her mouth so dry she felt as if she'd swallowed dust. She hated that she was trying to argue him into it.

'That was—an aberration.'

Small concession as that was, it gratified her. With her, he was different. He could be different. 'And so? Tonight can be an aberration, too.'

He shook his head slowly. 'Everything between us has been an aberration, Zoe.'

That didn't sound good, even as she recognised it for truth. Nothing between them had been normal, not even this. 'So what are you saying?' Her voice was small when she wanted it to be strident. 'Is that a no?'

'I…' He shook his head. 'I don't know what it is. I'm not—I'm not good at this.'

'Good at what?'

He gestured between the two of them with one impatient hand. *'This.'*

Everything, she supposed. Conversation. Closeness. A relationship. All the things she wanted, even if she knew she shouldn't. He glared at her, yet underneath the anger in his eyes she saw fear, and it made her heart contract.

'I'm not so good at it, either,' she said quietly.

He let out a huff of disbelieving laughter. 'Really.'

'Really.' She took a deep breath. 'What scares you more, Aaron—that you don't know how or that you want to?'

'*Want* to?

'Do you want to?' She stepped closer, gazing at him with all the honesty, hope and fear she felt. The words spilled out of her, needing to be spoken even though it might be the stupidest and most dangerous thing she'd ever said or done. 'Do you want something between us? I'm not saying I even know what it is.' She laid one hand on his arm and felt the muscles jump underneath her light touch.

'I'm not pushing for some—some kind of a relationship.'

'A relationship,' Aaron repeated tonelessly.

'But I feel something for you. And I think you feel something for me.' Zoe held her breath. Had she just ruined everything? Pushed too hard... again? Yet already she felt more for Aaron than she'd ever expected to, and it felt *real*. Not like the times before, when she'd forced a relationship because she'd been so desperate to prove she was lovable, that she wouldn't be rejected like before, and then of course she had been.

Except maybe she was still living in that fantasy world, because Aaron didn't say anything. He just stared at her, the darkness in his eyes and the grim set of his mouth making Zoe pretty sure he did not like having this conversation.

'I don't know what I feel,' he finally said, and Zoe felt incredulous hope unfurl inside her, start to bloom. It wasn't much of an admission, yet for a man like Aaron she knew it was huge. This was startling—and scary. It was new territory for him—and he was admitting it.

'That's okay,' she said, and squeezed his arm.

Aaron shook his head. 'I can't give you the things you want, Zoe.'

'How do you know what I want?'

'I could guess.'

'So what are you saying you can't give me?' She tried to stay light, but her heart was pounding. Already this conversation was out of both of their depths.

'I'm jumping ahead,' he said with another impatient shake of his head. 'This wasn't how I wanted to go about it.'

Now she really felt lost at sea, flailing with incomprehension. 'Go about what?'

Aaron took a deep breath and let it out in a shuddering, resolute sigh. 'Asking you to marry me.'

CHAPTER SEVEN

THE WORDS SEEMED to reverberate in the room between them, and vaguely Zoe realised this was the third time he'd shocked her with a suggestion—and this was the most shocking at all.

'You're joking,' she said, feebly, for of course he wasn't. Aaron didn't joke, and in any case the look on his face said enough. He looked like a man resolutely facing execution, which was not exactly the appearance one hoped for during a marriage proposal.

'You don't have to answer now,' he said steadily. 'Obviously, you need to think about it. But I've been considering what the best option is going forward—for us and for this child.'

'And you think it's *marriage*?'

His face hardened into implacable lines. 'Yes.'

Zoe shook her head, everything in her a jumble of mismatched feelings. She could not begin to sort out how she felt. 'But Aaron…'

'Like I said, you don't have to answer now. I probably shouldn't have brought it up, but it's been on my mind. Sleep on it.'

Protestations tumbled from her lips, her mind still whirling. 'But we don't even know if this pregnancy is truly viable yet.'

Aaron nodded, his gaze steady on her. He didn't seem remotely ruffled. 'And we don't have to get married tomorrow. We have time. Time to think.'

'You seem to have made up your mind,' Zoe observed numbly.

'Yes, but I realise it might be different for you.'

'Different?' Curiosity flared within her. 'How?'

He lifted one shoulder in a shrug. 'It's different for women.'

'That's a stereotype if I've ever heard one.'

He raised his eyebrows, a faint, sardonic smile curling his mouth. 'Are we really going to argue about this now?'

'You brought it up,' Zoe retorted, then closed her eyes and shook her head. 'I'm sorry. I'm shocked. I feel like you jumped a mile ahead of me.' To think a few moments ago she'd been nervous she was pushing too hard when all she'd said was she felt something for him. He'd responded with a marriage proposal.

But not with a declaration of love. Now she was clearly the one jumping ahead because obviously, *obviously,* Aaron was only talking about some kind of bizarre business arrangement.

'I'm sorry for springing it on you at this unfortunate hour,' he said tiredly. 'We can talk about it in the morning, when we're both a bit more rested.'

'That sounds like a good idea,' Zoe said shakily, and on leaden legs she headed for her bedroom. Aaron stopped her with a word.

'Wait.' She turned around, expectant, wary. 'I thought you were sleeping with me.' His eyes were dark, fathomless, intense. Zoe felt her heart beat hard.

'But I thought—' She stopped, for he simply held out his hand and after a second's uncertain pause she took it.

Lying in bed with him, with his arms tucked securely around her middle, his chin resting on her shoulder, should have felt strange. New, at least. Yet as she fit her body against him and felt his tension slowly start to ease Zoe knew it only felt right. Like coming home, which was ridiculous, yet she could not keep herself from feeling it. From wanting this and even more.

If she and Aaron married, every night could be

like this. Unless, of course, he'd meant some kind of temporary marriage…until their child was a certain age? Or maybe just a cold-blooded business arrangement, which certainly seemed his style, to give their child the security of his name? Not a real marriage—a marriage that involved sharing and commitment and love, the kind of marriage she still wanted and had been searching for, even if she wasn't quite sure she believed in it anymore.

She had no answers, yet the fact that she was even asking the questions made her realise she was seriously considering Aaron's proposal. She hadn't said no out of hand. She hadn't even thought it… which was a terrifying thought in itself.

Some time near dawn she must have drifted into an uneasy doze, for when she awoke Aaron wasn't in the bed and she could hear the shower running. She sat up, pushing tangles of hair from her eyes as she heard the shower turn off. Aaron came into the room with only a towel slung low on his hips.

'Good morning.' He gave her a rather brusque nod before reaching for his clothes. The towel dropped, and Zoe's mouth dried as she took in Aaron's naked body; his back was to her, so she could observe and admire the taut, muscular lines of his back and thighs. He was perfectly proportioned and unaccountably built.

'Did you sleep well?' he asked, no more than solicitous, and Zoe yanked her gaze away from her perusal of his butt.

'Not really. Did you?'

He turned around, now clad in boxers, and gave her a surprisingly wry smile. She loved his smiles, rare as they were. They transformed his face, his whole self. They made her realise there was more to this man than taciturn authority. 'Actually, I did. Better than I have in ages. I suffer from insomnia.'

She smiled back. 'Maybe you should try sleeping with someone more often.'

His gaze blazed briefly into hers before he turned away. 'Maybe I will.'

Zoe slid out of the bed and went for her own shower. By the time she emerged Aaron was in the kitchen, dressed in a business suit and slicing strawberries for their breakfast.

Zoe hesitated in the doorway of her bedroom as she watched him, his movement so precise, a faint frown of concentration settled between his brows. He did everything so seriously, as if it was a hugely important matter, even cutting up some fruit. She realised then that he never would have asked her to marry him lightly.

He must have thought about every angle, every possibility. He'd had every answer. She walked forward with a smile on her face and Aaron turned.

'Hungry?'

'Yes. I'm always hungry in the mornings. And eating helps the nausea.' She slid onto a stool by the breakfast bar and plucked a strawberry from the bowl. 'You're usually at work by now.'

'I need to leave in a few minutes, but I thought we should talk.'

She nodded, eyeing the lines of strain from nose to mouth that never seemed to leave him. 'You work too hard, you know.'

'Not hard enough.' He spoke matter-of-factly, and Zoe stared at him incredulously.

'How can it not be hard enough? You're a millionaire, Aaron. Or is it a billionaire?' She shook her head. 'What more do you want?'

His mouth thinned as he put the rest of the sliced fruit in the bowl. 'It's not important.'

'Not important? If I'm going to marry you, don't you think I should know the answers to these questions?'

He glanced up, his gaze hooded, blazing and swift. 'So are you going to marry me?'

The breath bottled in her lungs and she held his gaze, shaking her head slowly. 'I don't know.'

'But you're thinking about it.'

'Yes,' she admitted. 'How can I not?'

'You could have dismissed it out of hand.'

Zoe felt a blush heat her cheeks. Yes, she could have—should have, probably. What sane woman even thought about marrying a man she barely knew? Wasn't always sure she liked? And when she was, unfortunately, quite positive that he didn't love her?

And yet… They shared something. She'd felt it last night, when she'd told him as much and seen the confusion in his eyes. She'd felt it when she'd lain in his arms and known there was absolutely no other place she would rather be. She felt it now… even as her brain was screaming at her to stop, not to leap into a relationship—a *marriage*—that would surely hurt her in the end.

Yet still she considered it. *Hoped.*

Typical Zoe, her sister would say, leaping ahead to a fairy-tale ending after the first date. Except this time Aaron had beaten her to it.

Except she didn't think he was envisioning fairy tales.

'I could have dismissed it,' she answered, willing her blush to fade. 'Perhaps I should. After all, this is the twenty-first century. Most people wouldn't bat an eyelid at a child with unmarried parents.'

'No,' Aaron agreed tonelessly. 'They probably wouldn't.'

'So why do you think it's a good idea?' Zoe dared to ask. 'You have to admit, it's a pretty big leap.'

'Marriage is always a pretty big leap.'

He had a pat answer for everything, but he wasn't really telling her much. Telling her the truth. 'But most people who get married have dated. Known each other.' She swallowed, forced herself to continue. 'Love each other.'

Aaron's expression didn't change. The man was like a stone, Zoe thought. 'Most people,' he agreed.

'What are you, Switzerland?' She rolled her eyes. 'Stop being so damn neutral. This isn't some negotiation.'

'Yes,' he answered. 'It is.'

Zoe leaned forward. 'Tell me the real reason, Aaron, why you want to marry me.' She saw Aaron still and his face go even blanker, if that were possible. She knew she shouldn't have said that. Shouldn't have made it about her, because it so obviously, painfully, wasn't. 'I mean,' she clarified quietly, 'Why you think marriage is the right choice in our—situation.' Now she was talking like him. Situations and solutions. So unemotional, so heartless.

Aaron didn't answer for a long moment; he seemed to be considering his words carefully. 'Because anything else is just making the best of things.'

'Isn't that what we're doing? What we should be doing?'

He shook his head. 'What's the alternative, really, Zoe? Coming to some awkward custody arrangement, where I'll get to see our child every other weekend, maybe a Wednesday evening?'

'That sounds like an ideal situation for you,' Zoe couldn't keep from replying. 'An ideal *solution*. You get to be a dad, but it doesn't impinge on your lifestyle. Your work.'

He gazed at her, giving nothing away. 'You think that's what I want?'

'It's certainly what you have seemed to want,' Zoe answered evenly. 'You've never acted like you're thrilled about this, Aaron, or like you're dying to change nappies.'

He didn't reply, just turned to pour coffee into a thick ceramic mug. 'You're off coffee, aren't you?' he asked her, his back to her, and stupidly it touched her that he'd noticed.

'I'll have tea.'

He reached for tea bags, still not answering her accusations, for that was what it felt like—like she'd lobbed a few grenades right into the kitchen. And yet she knew it was true; Aaron had never acted like he was happy about this. About her. And she wanted him to be.

'Just because I didn't choose something doesn't mean I won't do what's right,' he finally said, handing her a mug of tea. 'Trust me on that.' There was something so grim about his tone that Zoe felt as if he must be speaking from experience, although she had no idea what it could be.

'I don't want you to marry me because you think it's right,' she said, stung by the implication. 'I don't want anyone to marry me for that reason. I want to marry—'

'For love,' he finished flatly. 'I figured.'

She let out a short laugh. 'Don't sound so disgusted.'

'I'm not disgusted. Resigned, perhaps.'

'To what?'

'To the fact that you would resist because of this. Because I don't love you.'

Ouch. She blinked, willing herself not to react. Not to feel the hurt that still rushed through her like water through a burst dam. Of *course* he didn't love her. It would have been ridiculous and frankly unbelievable if he had said he had. Wasn't she glad he could be honest, at least?

She stirred her tea, staring down into its fragrant depths. 'And it doesn't bother you? The whole love thing, or lack of it?' she asked, her gaze still fixed firmly on her tea.

'No.'

Of course he didn't offer any more explanations. Getting personal information from this man was like getting blood from a stone. 'Why not?'

A shrug, a sip of coffee. 'It's not something I've ever counted on.'

'*Love?* But you must have some love in your life, Aaron. I mean, if not a woman, then your family. Your brothers.' He stared at her without expression and, exasperated, Zoe continued, 'All right—your mother, then.'

'My mother lived her life in a state of intense depression and died when I was fifteen.' He took a sip of coffee and glanced away. 'Besides, Luke was her favourite.'

It was more personal information than he'd ever offered before, and she had a feeling he regretted revealing it. 'I'm sorry,' she said quietly. 'I didn't know.'

'Why should you?'

'Is that why—why you're not interested in a loving relationship now?'

'This is not a discussion I'm interested in having,' he answered flatly. 'Next you'll be getting out the crayons and asking me to draw a picture of my feelings. Don't psychoanalyse me, Zoe, and don't hope that somehow I'll change. I suggested marriage, but I won't pretend I love you, or that I'll ever love you.'

'Ever?' she repeated, trying to make light of it rather than burst into tears, which was what at least part of her felt like doing. 'What, are you incapable?'

'Perhaps.'

'You don't even want to give it a chance?'

'No.'

No hope, then. She swallowed, nausea roiling inside her that had nothing to do with morning sickness. 'So what kind of marriage are you talking about, then?'

'A partnership. Maybe even a friendship.'

'Maybe?'

'I don't really do friendship. But I can try.'

'You don't *do friendship*?'

He shrugged. 'I don't have friends. I never have.'

She blinked, shocked by his admission even though part of her wasn't really surprised. 'What a lonely life you've led, Aaron.'

'You're only lonely if you feel lonely.'

'And have you felt lonely?'

He stared at her without blinking for a long moment. 'I don't know,' he finally said, and she knew it was a confession, more of one than he'd wanted to make.

'So what do you envision this marriage looking like? On, you know, a daily basis?'

He shrugged. 'I have no idea. Something the way it looks now, I suppose.'

With him working sixteen-hour days and her wandering around the apartment when she wasn't at work. Except, of course, it would be different, because she would have a child. And a life; she wouldn't be in this awful limbo, waiting for something to happen.

Except, Zoe thought with cringing insight, she would be. She would be in an even worse, endless limbo, waiting for him to love her. Even if he'd just told her he wouldn't, ever; Zoe knew that herself. Knew she would keep wishing for it, trying to make it happen, and living on the thin vapour of hope until she had nothing left.

Was that what she wanted with her life? Could she even survive it?

'Obviously,' Aaron said dryly, 'That doesn't sound very appealing to you.'

Zoe forced a smile. 'Did my face give it away?'

'Pretty much. You looked horrified. Still do.'

She let out a weary sigh. 'Love is kind of a big thing, Aaron, to give up forever.'

'I know that. And I understand that a marriage between us will involve a sacrifice on your part.'

'And yours too, I imagine.' He might live a lonely life, but he still was a player, enjoyed affairs, flings. Although he hadn't actually *said* he would give those up…or if this partnership would be in name only and not in the bedroom.

'It's not the same for me,' he answered with a shrug. 'I'm not giving up on a dream.'

Zoe swallowed past the tightness in her throat.

'That is how it feels,' she admitted. 'And yet maybe that's all it ever was, ever will be—a dream.'

'Do you really believe that?'

'I don't know. I haven't found the fairy tale yet and I'm thirty-one, so…' She shrugged, spreading her hands. 'Maybe this is as good as it gets. My best offer.'

Aaron gazed at her steadily. 'Only you can decide that.'

'Well, thank you for that,' she said a bit tartly. 'At least you're not trying to emotionally blackmail me into doing the right thing for the baby.'

'I want you to be sure. This would be a permanent arrangement, Zoe. I won't sanction a divorce a couple of years down the road.'

'Too bad New York is a no-fault state,' she answered flippantly, and Aaron reached out and curled one hand around her wrist.

'Don't joke,' he said in a low voice. 'It's true I couldn't keep you from divorcing me if you really wanted to, but I could make it hellish for you.'

A chill entered her soul; this was an Aaron she hadn't seen before, at least not since their first encounter over the stupid phone. This Aaron was cold, calculating, even cruel. This was the Aaron she'd wondered at when they'd first met, the Aaron that had given her a faint frisson of fear. Now she felt it in full.

She yanked her arm away from him. 'Nice way to threaten me.'

'Just stating facts.'

'And is this supposed to help me decide in your favour?' she snapped, still unsettled by the low, deadly note she'd heard in his voice, seen in his eyes.

'It is what it is.'

'What if you want to divorce?' she threw at him and he barely blinked.

'Won't happen.'

'You can't say that.'

'Yes,' he answered. 'I can.'

Zoe let out a breath. 'Were your parents divorced?'

'No, but they probably should have been.'

She let out a sudden, wild laugh. 'A funny thing for you to say, considering how against it you obviously are.'

He shrugged. 'If you can't keep your vows, you shouldn't get married.'

Who in his parents' marriage hadn't kept their vows? she wondered. His father? Was that the cause of his mother's depression? She swallowed, forcing herself to ask the next question. 'So you would keep your vows?'

His nostrils flared, his eyes narrowing. 'Of course.' She'd offended him even by asking the question, she realised.

'You've been with a lot of women,' she pointed out. 'I can understand why you might be reluctant to give that up.'

'But I would.'

He hadn't denied that he was reluctant, she noticed. She glanced down at her tea once more. 'So this marriage—it would be real? I mean, consummated?'

'I don't think we have a problem in that area.' She looked up to see him smiling faintly, and she gave a rather silly smile back. Memories of that night tumbled through her mind again, not just the pleasure and excitement but the sudden intimacy of that moment when he'd driven inside her, looked in her eyes and she'd felt…

Complete.

'No,' she agreed. 'I don't suppose we do.'

They didn't speak for a moment, and in that silence Zoe felt her cheeks heat as memories flashed yet again through her mind, an incredibly vivid montage. She imagined that Aaron knew exactly what she was thinking, and with a thrill she wondered if he were thinking it too.

He turned away, setting his coffee mug down with a decisive clink. 'I need to get to work. Obviously, you'll have to think about it some more.'

'Yes.' She still had a thousand questions, questions that bubbled up inside her in an unholy ferment and other questions she didn't even know how to ask. So much uncertainty, unknowing…

'I'll see you tonight,' Aaron said. She watched as he reached for his blazer and briefcase, and then he was gone.

She spent the morning pacing the apartment, her mind buzzing, and then when she couldn't stand it anymore she went outside and walked through Riverside Park, ending up in a playground right on the Hudson. She sat on a bench in the drowsy early-autumn sunshine and listened to the creak of the swings and the squeak of the slide, watched toddlers with chubby fists chase butterflies and beg for ice cream from the stand by the gate. She tried to imagine herself in this same place in a year or two, with her round-faced child toddling along, and perhaps Aaron too, sitting next to her, smiling at the antics of their son or daughter.

She felt a smile bloom across her face as she

pictured the scene, the three of them a family, a child drawing them together in ways she could only barely imagine. She wanted that. She wanted to belong to someone, to feel a part of something bigger than herself. She wanted to scoop a child up in her arms and tickle his tummy. She wanted to lift her head and share a knowing smile with that child's father: *Aaron.*

She wanted it to be reality—and yet, without love, would it be enough?

She was so tempted to say yes to Aaron's offer, even as another part of her acknowledged just how much she'd be giving up.

And yet perhaps she'd given up on it already… Four failed relationships, four men who had walked away from her without a backward glance, one of them who had utterly broken her. Did she really want to keep trying? Maybe if she made herself accept Aaron's lack of love it wouldn't bother her so much. She'd stop trying to find the fairy tale and settle for reality instead. A good reality. Dreams might not be the best foundation for a marriage, and at least she knew he would be faithful, committed…

Sighing, she rose from the bench. She knew this

was not a decision she could make on her own. She needed to talk to Millie.

She called her from her mobile as she walked back to the apartment. Her sister answered on the first ring, her voice sharp with worry.

'Zoe? Where have you been? I haven't heard from you in over a week.'

'Oh.' Zoe sank onto a park bench and closed her eyes. 'Sorry about that. I should have told you…'

'Told me what? Where are you? What's happened, Zoe?' Millie's voice rose with each question. 'Are you in trouble?'

'No.' Zoe opened her eyes. 'Why do you think I am?'

'I—I don't.' Her sister sounded surprised, even guarded. 'But disappearing without telling me is kind of worrisome.'

'I'm living with someone.' This was not, Zoe reflected, how she wanted to begin this conversation. She should have been up front with Millie from the beginning, she supposed; her news was now going to come as an almighty shock.

'Living with someone? But you weren't even dating someone at my wedding not so long ago!'

'I know.' *And I'm not dating someone now.* Even

if she was contemplating getting married. 'It's… complicated.'

Millie let out a weary sigh. 'It always is, with you, sweetie.'

Zoe knew she shouldn't feel stung. She joked about her nightmarish love life all the time; when Millie had been in deepest grief, hearing about some of Zoe's dating disasters had been the only thing to make her smile. Yet now, with everything so uncertain and raw, Zoe did feel that sharp needling of hurt at Millie's assumptions—and she knew more was to come.

'So tell me,' Millie prompted. 'Who is this guy?'

Which part to say first? The pregnancy or the father? 'It's Aaron.'

'Aaron? Aaron who?'

Zoe almost laughed. 'Aaron Bryant, your brother-in-law.'

'What?' The word came out of Millie like an explosion. *'Him?* Zoe, he's such a—such a jerk!'

'Nice way to talk about family, Mills.'

'But you've met him! You've seen how he behaves. He's barely had the time of day for Chase or Luke for their entire lives.'

'He lives with a lot of pressure.' Zoe spoke instinctively, knowing it was true. She'd seen it in the taut lines of Aaron's face, the set of his shoulders and the shadows in his eyes. And, while she didn't know what the source of the strain was between Aaron and his brothers, she couldn't help but defend him.

'He's so not your type,' Millie said helplessly, and Zoe almost smiled.

'My type hasn't been a runaway success before.'

'Your type,' her sister answered tartly, 'has always been a guy who screws with you. Don't do it again, Zoe. Aaron will break your heart and he won't even care.'

She blinked at this blatant truth. 'He would care,' she said softly. But he would still do it.

Millie was silent and Zoe could almost hear her sister's mind spinning. 'When did this happen?'

'The night of your wedding, actually.'

'The night—? You mean—?'

'I'm pregnant, Millie.'

Another long silence, and this one was awful. Zoe wondered if Millie was thinking about her own daughter. 'I'm sorry,' she finally said and Zoe stiffened.

'I'm not. I want to have this baby.'

'You do? But—'

'But what?'

'Well, I'm surprised,' Millie said carefully. 'Your life isn't exactly—'

'That's just what Aaron said.'

'So you've told Aaron that you're pregnant?'

Zoe blew out a breath. 'Well, since I'm living with him, yes.'

'Why *are* you living with him? I mean, he doesn't seem the kind to—'

'He asked me.'

'Really.' Millie sounded completely disbelieving and, even though Zoe knew her sister's scepticism was certainly warranted, she still felt a stab of irritation. Was it so hard to believe that Aaron might want to be with her? That something between them could actually work?

'He wants to be involved,' she said stiffly. 'As a father.'

'Okay.' Millie was silent again, clearly processing this. 'You know we'll help you, Zoe—Chase and I. You don't have to rely on Aaron. I mean, if you need money or whatever.'

'I don't need money.' Zoe swallowed. This conversation was going all wrong. She felt wrong, like Millie was ruining something she hadn't even realised was precious. 'Actually, Aaron's asked me to marry him.'

Millie said nothing, which somehow was worse than if she'd exploded again. 'Millie?' she finally asked. 'Aren't you going to say something?'

'I don't know what to say.'

'You sound like Mum.'

'Sorry.' Millie let out a sigh. 'I mean, marriage— and you barely know him.'

'How long did you know Chase before you realised you loved him?' Zoe retorted. She knew it had been less than a week. She and Aaron had more history than that now.

'That's different,' Millie protested. 'That was Chase. And this is Aaron.'

'So? They're both Bryants.'

'Yes, but Chase is— Well, he's a good person, Zoe. He's funny and charming and I knew right from the beginning that he would never want to hurt me.'

'Well, guess what?' Zoe answered, and heard her voice shake. 'I know that, too. Aaron doesn't want to hurt me, Millie. He wants to do the right thing. Desperately.'

'I'm sorry. I know I must sound terribly judgemental—'

'Yes. You do.'

Millie sighed again. 'I just don't want to see you

hurt, Zoe. I love you, and I've seen too many guys put you through the wringer. Guys with a lot less money, power and arrogance than Aaron Bryant.'

'I'm not going to get hurt this time.' Zoe knew she was speaking with more conviction than she truly felt. 'I'm walking into this with my eyes open.'

'What do you mean? Does he—does he love you?'

And there was the hollow heart of it, Zoe thought, the bitter root. 'No.'

'So why—?'

'It's best for the baby.'

'And you believe that? When you know we'll help you—Mum and Dad too?'

'I don't want to be my family's charity case,' Zoe said quietly. 'But that's not why I'm thinking of marrying him. I want my own life, Millie. My own family. I've spent the last ten years chasing the rainbow and I'm starting to believe it doesn't exist.'

'It *does, Zoe.*'

'For you, maybe. But, knowing the way I am, the way I always insist on falling in love with the wrong guy, maybe it's better to have a relationship where that isn't even an option.'

'But how do you know that's how it will be?' Millie asked in a low voice. 'How do you know you won't fall in love with him?'

'I'll just have to keep myself from it,' Zoe answered, and she knew her sister heard the aching bleakness in her voice.

She was still mulling over the question when she went to her session at the community centre. She had Robert again today. Over the last few weeks he'd made a little progress, and had opened up a bit about the anxiety he felt at not seeing his father.

'He's just so far away,' he said quietly as he carefully coloured in a huge, endless ocean of blue on his paper. Zoe nodded in understanding. Robert's father had moved to California, farther than the little boy could even grasp, and yet he'd still feel the separation if his father lived in Brooklyn. Sometimes distance didn't matter. The orientation of your heart did.

And, whether Aaron was in California or on the Upper West Side, she might always feel as if he were an ocean away, Zoe thought as she cleaned up after Robert had left the centre. Could she live with that kind of emotional distance?

'Hello, Zoe.'

She turned in surprise to see the man in question standing in the doorway of the art room. 'What are you doing here?'

'I thought I ought to see where you worked.'

She smiled, unaccountably thrilled that he'd made the effort. 'Well, here it is.'

He took a step into the room, seeming to dominate the space, and glanced around at the child-sized tables, the buckets of markers and crayons, the spills of glitter and paint. 'Any breakthroughs today?'

'It's more about little steps.'

He nodded. 'I'd agree with that. I saw you working with that little boy.' He nodded towards the table. 'He seemed sad.'

'He is sad. Life's been tough for him lately.'

'And the drawing's helping?'

'I think so. It helps him to accept the way things are, and that it's okay to be sad.'

He nodded slowly. 'That's a big one, isn't it?'

Her heart lurched; she knew how difficult it was for Aaron to talk about his emotions. With a smile to show she was sort of teasing, she gestured to the tub of crayons. 'You could have a go.'

'Maybe I should. It seems to work.' He didn't move and Zoe waited, sensing he wanted to say something more. 'Zoe, I don't think I handled our conversation well this morning.'

'You don't?'

'I only mean to say…I *will* try.'

He gazed at her, looking both vulnerable and determined, and Zoe's heart squeezed. 'Try what?' she asked softly.

'Try to make this work between us. I'm not—I don't think I'm capable of loving someone. I've never…' He shook his head with a touch of the old impatience. 'That's never been a part of my life. But I want to make a marriage between us work. I want to make you happy, if you agree.'

'Oh, Aaron.' She blinked back sudden tears. His reluctant confession and barely made promise should hardly have moved her to tears, but it did, because she knew how much such intimacy cost him. How much he meant it.

'You've already decided, haven't you?' he said, and she knew from the flatness of his tone he thought she was turning him down.

'Yes, I have.' Zoe took a breath. 'I'll marry you.'

'You will?' Aaron looked so slack-jawed that she let out a trembling laugh.

'Surprise.'

'I—I thought you'd hold out,' he said. 'For love.'

'I've been holding out for love for ten years and I haven't found it yet.'

'I didn't think you were one to give up.'

I'm not. No, she could not think like that. She absolutely could not think like that, not if she wanted to have any chance at all of making this work. She needed to accept just how little Aaron thought he could give. She smiled and arched her eyebrows. 'Are you trying to convince me *not* to marry you?'

'No.' He took a step towards her. 'No, of course not. I'm just surprised.'

'Good surprised, I hope?'

'Yes.' He took another step towards her, and then another, and then he stopped, like he couldn't go any farther, or maybe because he felt he'd gone far enough.

A kiss would have been nice, Zoe thought. A touch. But Aaron stood on the other side of the room and just stared. 'We'll work out the details,' he said and she rolled her eyes.

'Just another business contract?'

'There are some similarities.'

She laughed, or tried to, because the tangle of emotions had knotted in her chest and suddenly it hurt to breathe. To think. What had she done?

What had she agreed to, committing her life to this man?

'Well, we have time,' she finally managed. 'I'm just over two months along. We don't have to rush.'

'No, of course not.' He cracked a smile then, a real one. 'But I'm glad, Zoe. Thank you.'

And just like that the knot dissolved and her heart started to melt. Dear Lord, she was in trouble.

But trouble felt good, she decided later that night as she slept once more in Aaron's arms. He'd surprised her by asking her to sleep with him again, and she'd accepted with rather alarming alacrity.

Still, she slept better than she had in weeks, only to wake in the middle of the night, the room drenched in darkness, a stabbing pain deep in her middle. She curled her legs up to her chest and then gasped as the pain knifed her again, worse than ever before.

Aaron stirred, his arms tightening around her. 'Zoe?' he murmured sleepily. 'Are you okay?'

'No!' she gasped as pain knifed through her again. Something was wrong. Something was really, really wrong. 'Aaron…'

He was up immediately, the covers rucked

around his waist as he went to switch on the light. Zoe's vision swamped and she thought she might vomit. Aaron stared at her, his face stark-white, his hand already reaching for the phone.

'Aaron!' she gasped again, and that was all she could manage as she fell back against the pillows, unconscious.

CHAPTER EIGHT

'It was an ectopic pregnancy.'

Aaron stared at the rumpled-looking doctor and tried to make sense of the words. 'Ectopic,' he repeated. He'd heard the word before, but he didn't know what it meant. All he knew was the last four hours had been hellish, from the moment Zoe had woken up in his arms, gasping with pain, and then fallen unconscious.

The call to 911, the ride to the ER in an ambulance, the endless wait in a fluorescent-lit waiting room—all of it had felt like a mindless blur until now, when he was finally going to find out what had happened to Zoe—and to his child.

'An ectopic pregnancy is one in which the embryo implants outside of the uterus,' the doctor explained. 'In this case, in Miss Parker's fallopian tube. The tube ruptured, and we had to operate to remove the damaged tube as well as the embryo.'

The embryo. Aaron blinked. He meant the baby.

Their baby was gone. Swallowing, he asked the question he knew mattered most. 'Is—is Zoe all right?'

'She'll be fine,' the doctor said with a tired smile. 'She's lost a lot of blood, and we're giving her a transfusion. She needs rest to recover, but she will. In a few weeks, a month, she should be fine.'

A *month*? Aaron passed a shaky hand over his face. 'May I see her?'

'She's sedated, but you can have a look in if you like. If you come back tomorrow, she should be awake and able to receive visitors.'

Aaron nodded and wordlessly followed the man down a long corridor to a hospital room. Zoe lay in bed, looking pale and small and so unbearably fragile. Her lashes feathered against her cheeks, and her breathing was slow and even, but faint, so faint.

Aaron reached out a hand to the wall to steady himself. He felt as if his whole world had shattered, exploded, in the course of a single night.

He barely remembered the ride back to his apartment; his mind was numb, blank. He stepped inside the penthouse and felt its emptiness, which he knew was ridiculous because Zoe had only been living with him for a short while. He was used to being alone. He *liked* being alone.

Except now he found he didn't. Now he found he felt empty and wretched, *lonely*. This was what loneliness felt like, he thought as he poured himself a double shot of whisky. It felt as if his whole world had collapsed around him and there was absolutely nothing left.

He tossed back the whisky and strode towards his study. Sleep would not come tonight. He powered up his laptop and stared resolutely at the screen. At least now he could focus on work; he could remain alone, he could do what he needed to do. He need never see Zoe again.

The thought made emptiness swoop through him, air whistling right through the place where he should have had a heart.

Eight hours later Aaron was back at the hospital, gritty-eyed and dressed for work. He'd bought some flowers; originally the florist had suggested a subdued bouquet of white chrysanthemums, but Aaron didn't want flowers meant for grief, and he didn't think Zoe did either. He chose lilacs, like the ones in her painting. He'd stared at it this morning as he'd drunk cold, black coffee, looked around his apartment and realised how she'd made it a home.

Their home. The thought made that empty space inside him ache.

Now he stood in the doorway of her room, the bouquet in hand, words bottling in his throat. She was sitting up in bed, the hospital gown emphasising the sharp bones of her clavicle. Her face was turned away from him.

'Zoe.' He spoke softly, but he could tell she'd heard him. She stiffened slightly, but didn't turn towards him. He took a step in the room. 'How are you doing?'

'Fine.' She faced him then, her face pale so the spattering of freckles stood out on her nose and cheeks. She smiled and shrugged, jolting Aaron out of his cautious approach. 'Why wouldn't I be fine?'

'A lot of reasons, I would think.' He put the bouquet on the table next to her. 'These are for you.'

'They're very pretty. Thank you.'

He gazed at her and tried to figure out what was going on in her head. He had no idea. Her eyes were dark and fathomless, her smile fixed. She folded her hands in her lap across the starched sheets.

'Admittedly, I feel a bit weak,' she told him. 'But

overall I'm okay. And, really, this is probably the best outcome, don't you think?'

'Don't say that.' He spoke with instinctive sharpness, a gut-level reaction.

'Why not? We were making the best of a bad situation, Aaron, and now we don't have to.'

He shook his head, the tightness in his chest taking over his whole body, making it impossible to speak. Finally he managed a few words. 'You wanted this baby.'

'Even so. You said it yourself—my life wasn't really set up for a baby. I wasn't really sure how it was going to work.'

You were going to marry me. He just shook his head. 'Zoe…'

She cut him off, her voice turning hard. 'There's no point pretending that this isn't the best thing for both of us.'

He stared at her helplessly, because even though he knew there might be truth to her words he didn't feel it. He didn't feel it at all. 'Don't say that, Zoe,' he said quietly and she lifted her face to stare at him with a blankness that made him ache all the more.

'Why not? It's true.'

'It's not true.' His voice was a low throb. 'I might

have said we were making the best of a—a situation, but you're still grieving. And I wish this hadn't happened.' He sat down next to her and reached for her hand. She pulled away. 'Zoe, please.'

'Do you?' she asked dully. 'Do you really wish this hadn't happened, Aaron?'

He blinked, cut to the quick by her question even as he recognised its validity. 'Of course I do. You almost *died*, Zoe.'

'And the baby? Aren't you a little bit relieved that you don't have to deal with that anymore?'

'No.' He blinked hard and swallowed past the tightness in his throat. '*No*. Zoe, whatever you think, I'm not that heartless, I swear.'

She lowered her head, her hair falling forward to hide her face. 'The doctor told me I might not be able to have any more children.'

He froze, fresh grief sweeping coldly through him. He couldn't think of a single thing to say. 'There must be ways,' he finally managed.

'Maybe with IVF, but I have a lot of scarring. The whole reason this happened in the first place was because of a burst appendix I had when I was thirteen.' She spoke dully, as if none of it really mattered. 'All the scarring *severely limits* my fertility, according to the doctor.' She held her fingers up in claw-like quotation marks, a horrible smile twisting her face.

'We can think about that later,' Aaron said steadily. 'The important thing now is to get you feeling better.'

'I'll never feel better.' Her voice tore on the words and she turned away from him. Aaron felt his control slipping away from him, if he'd had it at all.

'You will, Zoe, with time and rest. You *will*.' He took a deep breath and decided they both needed to focus on practicalities for a moment. The emotion in the room was palpable and thick, choking him. 'The doctor has said you need to rest for at least a couple of weeks.'

'I know. I can go to Millie and Chase's.'

'I have another idea.' She just stared, her face as blank as ever. 'I thought a change of scene might be—welcome. Get away from everything here. You could spend a few weeks on St Julian's. It's my family's private island.'

'In the Caribbean? I know. It's where Chase and Millie met.'

'Right.' He'd forgotten that. 'I have a private villa on the grounds of the resort. You could stay there, enjoy some sunshine, recover.' She didn't speak and Aaron continued awkwardly, 'I could stay with you for a few days. I'd have to get back to work eventually, but I could take some time off.' Still nothing. 'Zoe?'

'Fine.' She turned to face the window. 'Who am I to turn down a free vacation?'

'All right.' He felt gratified yet uneasy, because he knew Zoe had to be drowning in an ocean of grief. He didn't know how to access it, how to help her. He felt like he was drowning himself. 'I think you can be discharged tomorrow, so I'll arrange a flight.'

'Fine.'

'All right.' He hesitated, wanting to say something more, something of the grief inside him that he didn't like to probe too deeply, didn't even really understand. She was still stubbornly looking away from him, and with a little sigh he headed for the door. 'I'll see you tomorrow.'

No response. Yet as he started walking down the hall some impulse made him turn around, head back. As he came round in the door he saw Zoe holding the bouquet of lilacs to her face, her eyes closed, and something in him twisted. She let out a ragged sob, and without even thinking he started towards her, his arms outstretched.

'Zoe…'

She looked up, her eyes sparkling with both tears and fury. 'Go away,' she hissed. 'Leave me alone, Aaron.' She turned away again and, both shocked and hurt, Aaron dropped his arms. Without another word, he turned and left.

Hold it together. It was her mantra, her prayer. *Hold it together, because if you don't you will completely fall apart and there might be no getting you back together again.*

Drawing a deep breath, Zoe shoved the bouquet back on the bedside table. She blinked back the tears that had risen so readily to her eyes and felt a cold calmness seep through her once more. Good. This was what she needed. She was glad Aaron had gone. She needed him to leave her alone, because she could not keep it together with him near her, trying to be kind.

Twenty-four hours later, still feeling weak, achey and incredibly tired, Zoe boarded Aaron's private jet for St Julian's. They had barely spoken since he'd picked her up at the hospital and taken her in his limo to the airport, and Zoe was grateful for the reprieve. His attempts at kindness felt like salt in a raw wound, every smile or worried frown hurting her.

It hurt that he was now practically giving away the kindnesses and thoughtfulness she'd craved when she'd been pregnant and planning to marry him. And why? Because of his wretched sense of duty—or a labouring guilt?

Either way, she couldn't stand it. Her only defence was to feel numb, empty, even though she knew all those awful emotions—grief, rage, despair—lurked underneath that emptiness, like freezing water under the thinnest ice, and she did not dare touch the surface for fear those tiny hairline cracks would appear and she would drown in the depths below.

She'd become like Aaron, afraid of her own emotions. Hiding from them, because it was the only way she could cope.

'It's about a four-hour flight,' Aaron said as he took her elbow to help her manage the stairs up to the plane. 'There's a bedroom in the back,' he added as she stepped inside, distantly amazed by all the luxury: leather sofas, teak coffe tables and a sumptuous carpet that came up nearly to her ankles. She could hardly believe she was on a private jet…and she didn't even care. 'Do you want to rest?'

Zoe nodded. Rest was good. Rest meant sleep, which meant not talking, not even thinking. 'Yes, thanks. I'm still feeling pretty wiped out.'

'Of course you are,' Aaron murmured and, still holding her elbow, he led her to the bedroom in the back with a king-sized bed and en suite bathroom.

'It's like a hotel,' Zoe managed as she sank onto the silk duvet. 'A hotel in the sky.'

'And perfect for moments like these,' Aaron said lightly. 'Let me help you.'

She watched, surprised and yet still numb, as he sank to his knees in front of her. 'You don't have to,' she began as he slipped off her shoes.

'I want to,' he said in a low voice, and she wondered what this was. Atonement? Did he feel guilty, as if somehow he'd brought this on her, on both of them? He hadn't wanted their baby, and now they didn't have it anymore.

Illogical, she knew, and yet it was a thought that had crept into her mind all too often. With effort she slid her legs up onto the bed. 'I'm fine.'

'You keep saying that.'

Because, if I keep saying it, maybe I'll believe it. Maybe it will be true. 'I just want to sleep.'

'Okay.' She watched as Aaron peeled back the duvet and then, before she could protest, he lifted her as gently and easily as if she were a doll and placed her beneath the covers, tucking them over her with a tenderness she hadn't even known he possessed. She wished he didn't, because he was making everything so much harder.

She turned her face away, felt the starchy coolness of the pillow against her cheek, and closed her eyes.

'I'll let you sleep now,' Aaron said. 'I'll wake you up before we land.'

And then he was gone, the door clicking softly shut, and Zoe let herself tumble into blissful oblivion, the only thing she wanted now.

When she woke the room was dim, the curtains drawn against a blazing blue sky. Although she couldn't see him, Zoe could feel Aaron's presence in the room, knew he was watching her. She blinked, stirred, and he leaned forward, coming into her vision.

'We'll be landing in about half an hour.'

She nodded, and she felt Aaron's cool fingers brush a wisp of hair from her face and tuck it behind her ear.

Instinctively she turned away. 'Don't.'

'I'm sorry. Did I hurt you?'

Your kindness hurts me. She could hardly say that, couldn't explain even to herself why it did. Only that Aaron's thoughtfulness, his sudden sensitivity, felt like a knife twisting in her gut, in her heart.

'Do you want something to eat or drink?' Aaron asked when she hadn't replied to him.

'Tea,' Zoe managed and closed her eyes again. 'Please.'

Aaron brought her tea a few minutes later and left as soon as he'd handed it to her, which made Zoe feel both relieved and disappointed. How, she wondered, was she going to manage the next few days with him? Even those first days in his apartment hadn't been as awkward, as painful, as this.

Perhaps she should have gone to Millie and Chase's, yet even now that prospect made her insides sour. After her argument with Millie, she could hardly bear to slink back to her, a screw-up yet again. She knew Millie would have been kind, understanding, and would have never even have thought 'I told you so'. Yet even so…

Zoe couldn't do it. She would rather be here, even if it meant this unbearable awkwardness and tension with Aaron.

She finished her tea and tidied herself up, brushing her hair and even managing a bit of blusher and lipstick. She looked awful, she saw as she gazed in the mirror: pale and haggard, with vivid purple shadows under her eyes. Sighing, she turned away. Her appearance hardly mattered now.

Aaron was seated in the main area of the jet and Zoe came in and sat across from him. 'The airstrip is on the edge of the resort,' he told her. 'We'll have a car waiting for us. You should be settled in the villa within the hour.'

'Thank you,' Zoe murmured. He was making everything so easy for her.

Twenty minutes later they'd landed, and just as Aaron had promised a luxury sedan was waiting on the tarmac. He helped her inside, sliding in next to her, his thigh brushing hers before he murmured an apology and moved away.

Tears stung her eyes and she blinked hard. She hated how stupidly emotional she was being, how everything felt sad, like an ending, even that little, courteous rejection.

The villa was utterly amazing, as Zoe had known it would be. Set a little apart from the rest of the resort's lush grounds, its living room had sliding glass doors leading straight to the beach on one side, and a private terrace and pool on the other. There were three bedrooms, all luxuriously appointed, and a gourmet kitchen already stocked with food.

'I tried to order what you liked,' Aaron said. 'Tea, dairy-free ice cream… And, of course, you can order anything from any of the hotel's restaurants and it will be delivered.'

'It all sounds amazing.' And thoughtful, yet she supposed that shouldn't surprise her. Aaron had, in his own way, always been thoughtful. He considered every angle, every possibility. And now his kindness stung. *It's too late,* she wanted to cry. Scream. *It's too late. There's no future for us now; making me love you will tear me apart even more.*

'I think I'll just change,' she said, because her loose fleece and sweatpants—she'd needed comfortable clothing for the plane—felt too warm in the sultry tropical air.

'Of course. There are clothes in the main bedroom.'

He'd given her the master bedroom, and the wardrobe was full of brand-new clothes: sun dresses and swimsuits; shorts and capris; silky, expensive-looking T-shirts, all in the bright colours she loved.

A few minutes later she'd changed into a T-shirt and capris and came out to see Aaron at the dining-room table with his laptop. He'd changed into a polo shirt and cargo shorts, the most casual clothes she'd ever seen him in. He looked as good in them as he did in black tie, the shirt hugging the sculpted planes of his chest, the shorts riding low on his lean hips.

'Sorry.' He closed his laptop. 'I just needed to check in with the office.'

'It's fine.' When had Aaron ever apologised for working? It was what he did, who he was. She didn't want him to change—couldn't let him, because it would hurt too much. Everything about this hurt. 'I'll just go outside and relax by the pool for a bit.'

'It's after lunch time. Shall I bring you something?'

Zoe shrugged. She was a little hungry, although she couldn't rouse herself enough to do much about it. 'Sure. Thanks.' She turned her back on him deliberately, not wanting him to follow her out to the terrace.

He didn't, and as she stretched out on a sun lounger, the sound of the surf a pleasant background noise to lull her to sleep, she hated the confusing mix of disappointment and relief she felt yet again.

She must have dozed off, for she woke when Aaron came out onto the terrace with a tray of food.

'I got a little bit of everything,' he said, and set the tray on the table. 'Coconut shrimp, avocado salad, sliced pineapple and some grilled fish. What would you like?'

She leaned back against the lounger and closed her eyes; the sun was bright and white-hot against her lids. 'It doesn't matter.'

Aaron didn't answer, but she heard him serving the food, the clink of cutlery and porcelain and then the gentle press of his hand on her shoulder. 'Here.'

She opened her eyes and saw him looking at her with such blatant concern that her throat went tight. She took the plate.

They ate in silence, and even though the food was delicious Zoe only picked at it. Eventually she pushed it aside and rose from the lounger. 'I think I'll have a nap.'

Aaron gazed up at her, his own lunch only half finished. 'All right.'

Without another word, Zoe escaped the terrace

and Aaron's overwhelming presence for the sanctuary of her bedroom—and sleep.

Yet lying there in bed, with the bright tropical sunlight filtering through the curtains, she found she couldn't sleep after all. She kept seeing Aaron in her mind's eye, that surprising tenderness softening his features, lowering his voice, making him someone she couldn't stand. Because it would be so easy to turn to him for comfort, to fall even deeper in love with him. She'd been halfway to it when he'd been hard and cold, and she knew if she let herself weaken now it would seal that awful fate.

There was no baby, and therefore no future for them. Aaron was only acting out of solicitude and maybe even guilt; nothing else bound them together. Nothing at all.

It would be better if he just left, Zoe thought. Left her alone here, to sleep away the days, and somehow eventually try to forget everything that had happened.

She finally drifted into a doze and when she awoke it was evening, the light through the curtain now violet and hazy. Zoe rose from the bed and took a shower, hoping to rouse herself from the grogginess that had overtaken her.

She felt only a little better as she came out into the living room and saw Aaron stretched out on the sofa, asleep. She stopped, her heart juddering in her chest. He looked so much softer in sleep, the lines of his face smoothed out, a day's stubble darkening his chin.

She had a sudden, insane impulse to go to him, to curl into his solid strength and let him put his arms around her. Let him offer her the comfort she so desperately craved.

She didn't move.

His eyes flickered open and he stared at her, their gazes holding for a long, silent moment. Suddenly Zoe couldn't think, couldn't even breathe. She just stared and longed and finally Aaron spoke.

'Zoe,' he said quietly. 'I'm sorry.'

She froze, then forced herself to move past him into the kitchen. She poured herself a glass of water, her hand shaking.

She heard Aaron rise from the sofa and walk towards her. 'Aren't you going to say anything?'

'There's nothing to say.'

'I disagree.'

'Why would there be something to say, Aaron?' She heard her voice rise on a trembling note and took a deep breath. 'There's nothing between us anymore. We have no relationship, no future, nothing to talk about.'

He was silent and she didn't dare turn around. She didn't have the strength so much as to see the expression on his face, much less have this conversation. She *wouldn't* have it.

'I don't even know why you're here,' she continued, her voice rising again. 'Unless it's out of guilt.'

'Guilt?' Aaron repeated neutrally. Zoe turned around.

'Yes, guilt. Because you got what you wanted, didn't you? And you didn't even have to pay me a cent, never mind fifty grand.'

She saw Aaron flinch and knew she'd hurt him; she felt a savage twist of both remorse and satisfaction. She wanted to hurt him, wanted to push him away, even if she knew she was hurting herself in the process. 'You must be celebrating,' she continued, her voice turning into an awful sneer. 'Or at least you should be.'

'Do I look like I'm celebrating, Zoe?' Aaron asked quietly, his voice turning raw and ragged. 'Do you honestly think I'm happy about this?'

She scrunched her eyes shut and shook her head. She couldn't manage any more. She felt his hands curl around her shoulders and he slowly, purposefully drew her to him.

'Zoe, please stop fighting me. Please stop pushing me away. I want to help you. I want to see you through this.'

'Why?' she demanded, her voice choked with tears. With heaving effort she pulled herself away from him. 'So you can walk away with a clear conscience?'

'Because I care about you!' His voice rose in an almost-roar that had them both blinking in shock.

'It's too late, Aaron,' Zoe said after a moment, her voice flat. 'After everything…' She shook her head, a cold numbness thankfully stealing over her once more. 'It's too late for anything between us now.'

CHAPTER NINE

WHEN ZOE CAME out of her bedroom the next morning, having endured a sleepless, endless night, Aaron was dressed in a business suit. He shut his laptop and slid it into his briefcase.

'You're going,' Zoe said flatly, and he nodded.

'It seems for the best.'

Which of course it was. It was what she wanted, what she had been pushing him towards last night. Yet in the unforgiving light of day it still hurt—far more than it should.

'I'll have someone from the hotel check on you every day,' he continued, still busy with his brief-case. 'At least twice a day.'

'That's not necessary.'

'It is.' He cut her off, his tone relentlessly final. 'You were very ill, Zoe. You still are. You could have died, you know.' She heard a faint tremor in his voice and she closed her eyes, fought against the impulse to offer him her own apology, to beg him to stay.

'Even so.'

'Dr Adams said you shouldn't be alone,' he continued flatly. 'The only reason I'm leaving at all is because it's obvious I'm doing more harm than good by staying.'

Guilt speared through her, an awful, sharp-edged thing, lacerating everything it touched. She opened her mouth to say something—but what? How could she explain her own actions without telling him the truth—that she cared too much for him already, that her grief was so overwhelming she didn't how to deal with it, how to deal with *him*?

'Goodbye,' she finally whispered, and she knew that hurt him, too.

The rest of the day dragged endlessly, a monotonous paradise, before the lull was broken by a phone call from Millie.

'St Julian's is beautiful, isn't it?' she said lightly, although Zoe still heard the thread of anxiety in her sister's voice.

'How did you know I was here?'

'Aaron called me.'

'Aaron? I didn't think he was even on speaking terms with you.'

'He wasn't,' Millie answered wryly. 'But he's

desperate, and he thinks you need someone to talk to. He's worried about you, Zoe.'

Her throat closed up and she swallowed with effort, forced herself to speak. 'He has a guilty conscience.'

'What do you mean?'

Too late she realised she'd revealed too much. She would never tell anyone, much less her sister, about Aaron's initial offer. 'Never mind. It doesn't matter.'

'How are you doing?' Millie asked softly and her throat tightened again.

'I'm fine.'

'Oh, Zoe. You remember when I kept saying that, after Rob and Charlotte…?' Even now Millie had trouble talking about her husband and daughter. 'You're not fine. You're never fine when you suffer a loss.'

'A miscarriage is hardly the same,' Zoe answered. 'You've suffered far more than I have, Millie. I've always known that.'

'Is that what you think?' Millie asked quietly. 'That my grief is more than yours?'

It was always how she'd thought. How could she talk about her paltry problems—being dumped by her fiancé—when Millie had lost everyone and everything?

'Zoe,' Millie said, her voice gentle, 'grief is grief. And pain is pain. I would never presume to think my experience somehow trumps yours.'

But it did, Zoe filled in silently. It always had. It had been silently and implicitly understood in her family that nothing she ever endured would compare to what Millie had happen to her. She had never attempted to try, had armoured herself with insouciance instead. It was how she'd handled life: lift your chin and laugh it off. Except now she couldn't. Now she was raw, exposed and vulnerable, hating how much weakness was on display.

'You shouldn't be there alone,' Millie said when Zoe hadn't said anything—couldn't. 'Don't close yourself off, Zoe. I know how that goes. It's okay for a little while, and sometimes it's what you need. But you can't hide forever.'

'This is hardly forever.'

'How long are you planning on staying on St Julian's?'

'I don't know.' She didn't have any reason to return to New York, she thought. She no longer worked at the café, and Aaron had arranged a month's leave of absence from the community centre.

And, even when she was able to resume her work as an art therapist, what about her life? Her friends? She'd kept so much from them over the last few months, and now she felt so changed from the carefree, insouciant woman—*girl*—she'd been before.

'Zoe?' Millie prompted gently. 'Maybe you should come back to New York. You could stay with me and Chase.'

'No.' The word came out too quickly, involuntary and immediate. Instinctive. 'That's very kind of you, Millie, but I'm a grown woman. I need to stand on my own two feet.' Even if she wasn't doing that now.

'Then perhaps you should reach out to Aaron,' Millie said after a moment. 'I wouldn't have said this when we talked before, but he cares about you, Zoe. I could tell. He's really worried about you.'

'I can't.' It was all she could manage.

'Is there something I don't know about, something about your relationship?'

Zoe closed her eyes. 'We don't have a relationship.'

'I thought you were thinking of marrying him.'

'That was when there was a baby.' She dragged a breath into her lungs. 'When there was a reason.'

'And now?' Millie asked quietly.

'There's nothing.'

'It didn't seem that way when I talked to Aaron.'

'All right then, there's not enough.' He would never love her. Strange, how she'd convinced herself it hadn't mattered when she'd been pregnant. Now, with the nothingness that had replaced her hope, she realised how much it did. How much she needed it.

'Maybe you should give him a chance,' Millie suggested.

'You're the one who said he was a big jerk,' she snapped. 'And that he'd break my heart and not even care.'

'Has he?' Millie asked quietly.

'No!' *Because I won't let him.*

'Oh, Zoe…' Millie sighed. 'I just don't want you to be on your own. What if—what if I came down? Spent a few days with you? It could be… Well, I won't say fun.' She let out a wobbly laugh. 'But it would be good to see you. I feel like I haven't seen you properly since I got married.'

'I know.' And, even though she'd been deliberately avoiding Millie for most of that time, Zoe knew then that she missed her sister. The thought of seeing her again, having her sweep in and somehow rescue her was tempting—but impossible.

'I miss you, Mills,' she said. 'And I'll see you when I get back. But I need to be alone right now.'

'I don't like the thought of you out there by yourself.'

'You came here by yourself,' Zoe objected. 'Remember? And met Chase.'

'Are you hoping to meet a Chase?' Millie teased gently.

'There's only one Chase.' And there was only one Aaron. With a pang Zoe knew which one she wanted to be with.

Aaron spent the flight back to New York focused on work. He forced himself not to think of Zoe, of the accusations she'd spat at him like bullets. And like bullets they'd wounded him, made him bleed. *Did* he care about her now because he felt guilty? It almost seemed like the easy answer when the truth was far more damning.

He cared about her. Full stop. Forget about what they'd been planning before. He cared about her, and it terrified him.

Resolutely he turned back to his work. A mysterious shareholder was quietly buying up stocks in Bryant Enterprises, and Aaron had no idea who it was. Still, he sensed the danger; he'd always sensed the danger, always felt as if he were teetering on the edge of the precipice of disaster. Bankruptcy. Ruin. Shame.

The legacy of his father, the inheritance he'd been given and hidden not just from the world, but his own family. The shame he didn't want anyone to discover.

Halfway through the flight, he broke down and called Millie. It was an awkward conversation, but a necessary one. He didn't want Zoe to be completely isolated and alone. She needed someone, even if it wasn't him.

His mobile phone rang as he landed in New York. Glancing at the luminous screen, Aaron saw that it was his brother Chase, no doubt checking up on him after his phone call to Millie.

'Chase.'

'Hey, Aaron. How's Zoe?'

'Not all that great, as you probably know from your wife,' Aaron answered tersely.

'Millie's worried about her.'

'Of course she is. Zoe has gone through a very difficult time.'

'She thinks she shouldn't be alone.'

Aaron gritted his teeth. Like he needed to be told. 'I agree.'

'So?' Chase prompted. 'Why aren't you there?'

Aaron felt his fingers ache from gripping the phone so tightly. 'Because she doesn't want me there.'

'I don't think Zoe is in a position to know what she wants.'

Aaron felt a tiny flicker of doubt—or was it hope? 'She seemed pretty sure,' he said gruffly.

'You said yourself she's going through a tough time. She's grieving, Aaron. She's probably not making sense, even to herself.'

'I don't know,' Aaron said after a moment, and he heard how uncertain he sounded. And he never sounded uncertain, never showed any weakness or doubt. 'Look,' he said in a stronger voice, 'it's none of your business anyway.'

'Zoe is Millie's sister, so that makes it my business,' Chase answered. 'And you're my brother. Aaron, go back. Help her.'

Aaron closed his eyes, felt his throat thicken. He swallowed and forced himself to speak. 'I don't know how.'

'Then tell her exactly that,' Chase said gently. 'I think she'll understand.'

One of his staff had come into the main area of the plane, ready to assist. Grimly Aaron tossed his phone aside. 'We'll have to refuel,' he said. 'And then we're heading back to St Julian's.'

Zoe sat curled up in an armchair in the living room of the villa, the sliding glass doors open to the beach. A gorgeous sunset was streaking across the sky in technicolour glory, sending melting rays of gold and orange over the placid sea, yet she barely noticed it.

She'd spent one day alone and she was ready to climb the walls. Climb out of her own skin, because she couldn't stand it anymore. Couldn't stand herself. She drew in a shuddering breath and forced the emotion back. She couldn't deal with it, would never be able to deal with it.

She heard the door open and looked up, expecting one of the staff returning to clear away the dinner she'd barely touched. Instead her heart seemed to stop right in her chest, for Aaron stood in the foyer looking tired, rumpled and utterly wonderful.

Zoe swallowed, half rising from her chair. 'What are you doing here?'

Aaron's gaze narrowed in on her and he tugged at his tie. Funny, how he always wore suits yet he always took his tie off as soon as possible, shed it with a flicker of relief as if he was finally just a little bit free.

'What am I doing here?' he repeated as he came towards her. 'The real question is, why did I ever leave?' He dropped to his knees in front of her. 'I'm sorry, Zoe. I never should have left you alone, not even for a minute.'

She stared at him incredulously, longing to touch him, yet afraid to. 'You must have flown to New York and straight back again.'

'That's exactly what I did.'

She shook her head, her throat thick with tears. 'I was trying to make you leave.'

'I know you were.'

'Then why—why did you come back?'

'Because I'm not going to let you push me away. Because I want to be here, with you, working this out together.'

'I shouldn't have—I shouldn't have said those things to you.'

'Why did you?' Aaron asked quietly. 'Are you angry at me?'

Zoe opened her mouth to deny it and then realised she couldn't. 'I don't know,' she whispered. 'I know I shouldn't be.'

Aaron shook his head, his eyes dark. 'Maybe you should.'

'Why?'

'Because,' he said bleakly, 'I didn't want our child at the start. At least, I convinced myself I didn't.'

'That has no bearing on what happened,' Zoe answered, her voice wobbling noticeably despite her effort to sound reasonable. To feel it. 'It's not—it's not like you caused the pregnancy to be ectopic, Aaron.'

'I know that.' He let out a long sigh. 'But logic doesn't always trump emotion.'

'I thought it did with you,' Zoe said with a small, watery smile.

'I always meant for it to. But lately…' He shook his head again, his eyes dark and full of shadows, yet Zoe saw more honesty reflected in them than she'd ever seen before. 'I don't know what I feel, Zoe. And I don't know what you feel. Maybe you want me to go, but I want to be here. With you.'

She felt her throat thicken with tears and she blinked hard. 'I want you to be here,' she whispered. 'But I don't even know why, or what that means. I don't know anything, Aaron.'

'I wouldn't expect you to,' Aaron said, his voice rough with emotion. 'You're still grieving, Zoe. You're keeping it all inside, bottling it up. Trust me, I know how that goes. But you've got to let it out.'

Her throat was so tight now she could barely speak. She blinked hard, willing the tears back. She might have admitted more to this man than she'd meant to, but she would not cry in front of him. She would not fall apart, because she knew there would be no putting herself back together again. At least not the way she'd been, the way she wanted to be again.

The way she knew she could never return to.

'No,' she finally said, the word strangled on a sob. *'No.'*

'Zoe.' She felt Aaron's hands on her shoulders; she still wouldn't look at him.

'Don't,' she whispered. 'Please don't. I can't.'

'Why not?' he asked gently. His hands were still curled around her shoulders and he was slowly, inexorably drawing her towards him. Zoe didn't have the strength to resist.

'Why are you doing this?' she protested brokenly. 'You're the one who told me you hated all that emotional stuff. Quantifiable results, remember?'

'Maybe I've changed.'

'You *haven't.*' She didn't want him to change. Didn't want to consider what that meant for her, for her heart.

He had drawn her to him, and now he pulled her onto his lap. Zoe went woodenly, unable to resist, yet still possessing enough strength not to curl into him as she wanted to, accept the comfort he was offering.

'Zoe,' he said quietly. 'I'm sorry.'

'No.'

'I'm sorry I hurt you when I offered you that money. I'm sorry I didn't give us more of a chance when I should have.'

'No.'

'And most of all I'm sorry for the loss of our baby. I wanted that child, Zoe. I didn't even realise how much until—' He stopped, his voice choking, and the tears she'd only just managed to hold back finally fell, coursing down her cheeks in a hot river as she shook her head, still trying to deny his words, the effect they were having on her.

All her defences were crumbling. Her heart was

laid bare, weak, trembling organ that it was—defenceless, vulnerable.

'I'm sorry,' he whispered, and he wiped the tears from her cheeks, his arms around her, holding and protecting her. 'I'm so sorry,' he said again, a plea, a promise. 'I'm so, so sorry.'

Zoe didn't answer. She couldn't, for now that the tears had fallen the grief she'd locked deep inside came pouring out; her body shook with sobs and she buried her damp face in the warmth of Aaron's neck as she let her sadness overtake her.

She didn't know how long she cried. Time ceased to matter or even exist as Aaron held her and she poured out her heart. Eventually she stopped, utterly drained, yet feeling more replete than she had in a long time. She pulled away from him a little, wiped her face. 'I suppose I needed that.'

'I think you did.'

Yet now that she'd let the sadness out she didn't know what was left. She felt empty and, while it didn't feel too bad now, it still scared her. The future scared her, stretching endlessly ahead, and even though she craved the warmth and comfort of Aaron's arms she knew she couldn't stay there. Didn't even belong there.

'Thank you,' she said. 'For—for understanding.'

She tried to slip off his lap, but his arms tightened around her and he wouldn't let her go.

'Don't, Zoe.'

'Don't what?'

'Don't push me away again.'

She forced herself to say the truth. 'It's not as if there's any future for us, Aaron.'

'Isn't there?'

She stilled, too shocked to form words. 'What do you mean?' she finally managed in a whisper.

'I know we came together out of expediency.'

'Making the best of a bad situation,' Zoe reminded him, her voice sharpening just a little.

Aaron acknowledged this with a nod. 'But I still feel something for you, Zoe, just like you told me I did. I haven't been able to admit it even to myself, but you saw it. You saw the truth in me.'

'Wishful thinking on my part,' Zoe managed and he shook his head.

'No, it's the truth. I care about you, and I don't want to walk away just because things have changed.'

Zoe didn't answer. Her mind whirled with this new information, because in all the scenarios she'd foggily envisioned she had never once imagined this. She was the one who fell too hard, too fast, who threw herself into relationships, desperate to make them work, to prove she could make them work. And Aaron had made it all too abundantly clear that he didn't do relationships. Didn't do love. Had he really changed that much? Had she?

'Say something,' Aaron said softly as he brushed the remnants of tears from her eyes. 'Tell me what you're thinking.'

'I don't know what to think. I never expected you to want more from me. Frankly I thought—I thought you'd be relieved.'

'Which is why you were angry at me,' Aaron surmised. 'Well, in all honesty, I expected to be relieved. I even wanted to be because, hell, that's easier. But I'm not, Zoe.' He touched her chin with his fingertip and angled her face towards him. 'I can't promise you anything, because I don't know what I'm capable of. I haven't had a serious relationship with a woman—ever.' He let out a shaky laugh. 'That sounds rather grim, doesn't it?'

'Honestly? Yes.' Zoe managed a smile. 'But I'm glad you're admitting it.'

'But I want to try,' he said softly. 'With you.'

Zoe thrilled to hear the words yet, whether it was a thrill of excitement, joy or just fear she didn't know. Probably all three. She knew herself, knew that if she entered a relationship with Aaron, a proper one, she'd fall fast and hard as she always did. Faster and harder, even, because already this man had stirred up way too many emotions inside her. Already she knew she felt more for him—far more—than she'd ever felt before.

And if she fell and Aaron didn't? If he tried and failed? He hadn't even mentioned love, and Zoe was feeling too raw and exposed already to bring it up. Could she survive that all-too-likely scenario?

'I'm afraid,' she said quietly. 'I don't want to get hurt, Aaron.'

'I know.' He said nothing else, made no promises, just as he had said he wouldn't.

She couldn't do this. Couldn't risk so much, not when she'd lost so much already. She might be healing, but the scars were livid, fresh and still so very painful.

'I always have such bad timing,' Aaron murmured as he touched a fingertip to her eyelash, where another tear was already forming. 'I shouldn't have said all this now, when I just got here and we've barely talked. I'm sorry.'

'Stop apologising,' she said with a little smile. 'I think you must have said more sorries tonight than you ever have in your whole lifetime.'

'I have,' he admitted. 'I never say sorry. I never admit I'm wrong.'

'Why not?'

He thought for a moment. 'Because admitting it is showing weakness and I don't want to be weak.'

'Telling someone you want to be with them could be seen as weakness too,' Zoe pointed out. Aaron met her gaze steadily.

'I know.'

Her heart seemed to turn right over. He really was trying. Really was laying himself bare. How could she turn away from that? How could she keep her own heart intact when Aaron was trying to offer his own? Or at least as much of it as he knew how to.

She took a shuddering breath. 'Aaron...'

'Don't answer me now,' he said, pressing a finger against her parted lips. 'You need to think. Rest. Recover. All I ask is that you let me stay here with you.'

She nodded, his finger still against her mouth. With a small smile he traced the outline of her lips with the tip of his finger. Zoe felt a little pulse of longing deep in her belly, a jolt to her system, reminding her that she was awake, alive.

'Then we should both rest. Together, if you'll

have me. I've missed sleeping with my arms around you.'

She smiled, blinked hard. 'I've missed having them around me,' she whispered.

Silently Aaron led her to the master bedroom. As they got in bed Zoe hesitated for a moment, frozen in her loneliness and fear, before Aaron's arms came around her and her body reacted, instinctively knowing what to do. What she needed. She nestled into his embrace, her legs twining with his, her arms coming around his middle, glorying in the feel of him, hard muscle and hot skin.

Once again she was home.

CHAPTER TEN

AARON WOKE UP with Zoe's hair trailing across his bare chest, his hand cupping the warm fullness of her breast. He went immediately and painfully hard, even as he felt a thrill of both terror and joy.

This was so unbearably unfamiliar, so out of his control, and yet already so necessary and even vital. Nothing he'd said to her last night had been planned or expected. Every word out of his mouth had shocked him as much as he thought it had her: *All I ask is that you let me stay here with you... Maybe I've changed... I want to try...with you.*

He wasn't sure if he believed any of it, if he *could*. He'd lived his life in determined solitary independence, had wanted and needed to. The lessons he'd learned from his father went soul-deep: *don't trust anyone. Don't need anyone. Don't be weak.*

And yet his father had broken all his own rules, rules he'd drilled into his oldest son from the age of five—a realisation which had made Aaron only more determined. He wouldn't be like that. He'd take his father's lessons to heart and he'd live them. Perfectly.

Yet now he was breaking every rule spectacularly—and why? Because the few weeks he'd spent with Zoe had been the most awkward, intimate and wonderful of his whole life—and he wanted more. Even if it terrified him.

He felt Zoe stir in his arms and he glanced down at her, saw the fog of sleep in her eyes replaced with a wary smile. She wasn't sure of this either. Last night had been intense, with the tears, the honesty and the grief, but this was something else entirely. This was a beginning—but of what?

'Good morning,' he said, his voice a morning rasp.

'Good morning.'

'Sleep well?'

'Actually, yes.' She stretched and then curled back into him, sending a kick of lust ricocheting through him. He knew, what with the complications of the ectopic pregnancy, sex was out for at least a few weeks. His body, however, didn't seem to have received that memo. 'Did you?'

'Yes,' he admitted, because honestly he'd never

expected to like sharing his bed, for it to feel so good. So right.

'And now?' Zoe asked softly, and he saw all the uncertainty in her eyes. Uncertainty about him.

'I thought you might be tired of kicking around the resort,' he said.

'Okay…'

'So we could go sailing.'

A smile tugged at her mouth. 'You have a boat?'

'Yep.'

'That sounds wonderful,' she said, and Aaron's heart swelled with an emotion he could not name.

An hour later they were on the water, the sea placid and shimmering with a brilliant morning sun. Zoe sat on the cushioned seat in the stern of the boat, her legs tucked up to her chest, her face tilted to the sun. She'd pulled her hair back into a ponytail but tendrils and wisps had escaped, turned wild and curly by the sea air.

Aaron loved looking at her, loved seeing her relaxed and happy. He felt his heart swell again, and this time he knew it was with hope. She must have felt him gazing at her, for she lowered her head, raising one hand to shield her eyes from the glare of the sun, and turned to him with a smile.

'Do you know, I've actually never been on a sailing boat before?'

'Never?' They were in for a good run and so Aaron took the opportunity to join Zoe in the stern. 'How come?'

She shrugged. 'I was never a very sporty girl. Books and art were more my thing. But I have to admit, this is pretty amazing.' She glanced at him, curiosity flaring silver in her eyes. 'Did you Bryant boys all learn to sail at around the age of two?'

'More like six.' He sat down next to her, his thigh nudging her hip and sending a painful flare of awareness through him. It was going to be a tough day for his libido. 'We had a house out in the Hamptons, right on the Sound.'

'Had?'

This was somewhat dangerous territory, he realised. He didn't like talking about his childhood, the mistakes his father had made. 'It was sold when my father died.'

'When did your father die?'

'Ages ago, when I was twenty-one.' Just old enough to take the reins of Bryant Enterprises and realise how tightly he'd have to hold on to them.

'I'm sorry,' she said quietly. 'It must be hard, not to have either of your parents alive.'

He shrugged. 'It's been a long time.'

'A long time on your own. Why aren't you close to your brothers?'

Another shrug; he really didn't like talking about this. Was this what relationships were, all this honesty and intimacy, like peeling back your skin? No wonder he'd avoided them for so long.

'Aaron.' She laid a hand on his arm. 'I'm not trying to pry, you know. I promise I won't psychoanalyse. I just want to get to know you. And I want you to get to know me.' He could think of ways of getting to know her that did not involve such messy questions or any conversation at all.

With a sigh, he nodded. 'I know. I'm just not used to…talking about things.'

'I realise.' She gave him the glimmer of a smile. 'You can ask me some questions, if you want.'

'What made you go into art therapy?'

'The practical answer is that I knew I would never make it as an artist professionally, but I still wanted to do something related to art. The emotional one is that I like helping people, and being useful.' She gave a little laugh that sounded to Aaron like it had a bitter edge. 'Funny, really.'

'Why is that funny?'

Now she was the one shrugging, her gaze sliding away from his. 'I don't know. I suppose I'm not considered to have lived a very productive life.'

He frowned. 'Says who?'

'Put me next to Millie, with her super-important career and her completely together life, and I look pretty—useless.' She let out another quick laugh then shook her head, the movement almost frantic. 'Which is a terrible comparison to make, I know, because Millie's been through a lot and I can hardly discount—' She stopped suddenly, pressing her lips together. 'Oh, it doesn't matter anyway.'

Aaron stretched his legs out. 'Obviously it does.'

'Obviously?' she repeated, arching an eyebrow. 'Are you going to play psychologist on me, Aaron? Because that so does not seem your style.'

'You're the therapist,' he answered with a smile.

'Right. Maybe I should draw myself a picture.'

'Now you sound as cynical as me.'

She laughed, the sound ending on a sigh. 'No. I suppose I've always had a bit of an inferiority complex when it comes to my sister. Millie doesn't make me feel that way—not for a minute. It's more my parents. And myself.' She lapsed into silence, frowning as she gazed into the distance.

Aaron knew he should get up and tack but he was reluctant to abandon this conversation. Zoe was sharing more with him than he'd expected, and to his own surprise he found he wanted to know. 'So your parents wanted you to be a hedge-fund manager?'

'Didn't yours?' she flashed back, and he tensed. So they were back to him. He should have known he couldn't avoid personal questions for ever, or even for ten minutes.

'They certainly did.'

'Were you always meant to take over Bryant Enterprises?'

'Always.' He did not have a memory in which that expectation had not weighed heavily on him; it had nearly crippled him.

'What about your brothers?'

'They were meant to have responsibilities, as well. Luke was in charge of the retail division until a few months ago.' He still felt a frisson of shock that Luke had just given it all up, walked away from Bryant Enterprises and all that it meant. He was free. 'And Chase was disinherited by my father when he was nineteen.'

'Ouch. Why?'

'He screwed up one too many times. He was a bit of a wild kid.'

'And you?' Zoe asked softly. 'You were meant to be in charge of it all?'

'That's about it.' He tried to speak lightly but somehow his throat became constricted and he felt a welling of emotion in him that he didn't understand. Why did this woman wrest emotions from him, like drawing out poison? He felt it seep out of him, infecting everything, leaving him weak.

Zoe laid a hand on his arm; her skin was soft and warm from the sun. 'You don't like your job, do you?' she asked quietly.

'I hate it.' The words slipped out before he could stop them, and the vehemence with which he spoke surprised them both. It shocked him, really, and he felt a scorching rush of shame that he could have been so weak to admit such a thing, or even to feel it. That he could have betrayed his father, his family, so easily—and to a woman. Hadn't he learned anything from his father's mistakes?

Quickly Aaron slipped from the seat and walked back to the bow of the boat. It was time to tack.

Zoe watched Aaron walk away from her, every muscle in his body taut with tension. He'd said too much, she thought with a sigh. At least, he felt he had. She sat there, the sun still streaming over her, and let him go. Maybe he needed a little distance.

She knew her fatal tendency in relationships was to push. Demand or beg, it didn't matter which, but she got desperate and needy and no one liked that, not even herself. It was a legacy from Tim's betrayal, that she insisted on believing in love even as all her history said otherwise.

She watched Aaron do something with the sail—she really didn't know a thing about boats—and admired his long, lean torso, the wind pressing his polo shirt hard against the muscles of his chest. He squinted in the sun, his dark hair ruffled by the wind, and Zoe felt a surge of longing so deep and powerful it left her aching. The no-sex thing was going to be hard.

Dr Adams had told her she needed to have a check-up before he gave the all-clear, and since her surgery Zoe hadn't given it so much as a thought. Sex had been just about the furthest thing from her grief-stricken mind. Now, however, even though the grief was still there and always would be, she felt a fresh desire roll through her and remembered just how good sex with Aaron had been. Making love.

Would it be different, now that they cared more about each other? The thought sent another thrill ricocheting through her. It would be even more intense, more wonderful, more everything.

Smiling at the thought, she rose from the bench and joined him at the sail.

'I have no idea what you're doing,' she remarked and Aaron raised his eyebrows.

'Do you want a lesson?'

'Not particularly. I like watching you, though. You look all manly and heroic.'

He let out a short laugh, shaking his head. Zoe was surprised and a little bit touched to see a faint blush tinge his cheekbones with colour. He was a man of authority and power, yet also one unused to receiving compliments, even teasing, lighthearted ones.

They kept the conversation casual as Aaron managed the sail, and eventually navigated the little craft to a sheltered cove on the other side of St Julian's.

He brought out a picnic basket and laid a blanket on the sun-warmed deck of the boat. Zoe stretched out on it while Aaron served her delicacies from one of the resort's restaurants—calamari and coconut shrimp; plantain accras; fritters; baked goatcheese. They washed it all down with champagne, and ate succulent slices of fresh guava, papaya and passionfruit for dessert.

'So how did you end up with a whole island to

yourself?' Zoe asked as they ate, gazing out at the secluded side of St Julian's, the dense foliage fringing a white sand beach.

'Not exactly myself,' Aaron answered. 'The island is owned jointly by my brothers and me.'

'Even Chase?'

'Even Chase. The island belonged to my grandfather and he left it directly to the three of us.'

'Has it been in your family forever?'

'Hardly. The Bryant fortune isn't that old. My grandfather made most of it.' He lapsed into a sudden silence, his eyes narrowing as he gazed into the distance.

'And you and your father just added to the coffers?'

A pause, telling in its length. 'Something like that.'

Zoe took a breath, wanting more. Wanting to understand this man she was just beginning to realise was unsettlingly complex. 'Why do you hate your job, Aaron?' she asked quietly.

He tensed but said nothing. Zoe waited. She really didn't want to press, but neither was she willing to let it go. If they were going to attempt some kind of relationship, she needed more. She needed to know him.

'Hate was probably too strong a word,' he finally said—his voice deliberately mild, Zoe thought. 'I didn't choose it, put it that way.'

Zoe considered this. When he'd said he hated it, she'd felt those words come from somewhere deep inside him, somewhere she didn't think he accessed all that often. And she was just about a hundred percent certain they were true.

'If you hadn't been born a Bryant,' she asked after a moment, 'what career path do you think you would have taken?'

Aaron shrugged. 'Who knows. I never thought about it.'

'Never?'

'Never,' he said flatly.

'Is that what you don't like? The lack of choice?'

'What I didn't like,' Aaron said, the words coming sharp and sudden, 'was being lied to. Over and over again, so my whole life was built on nothing but deception.' He shook his head and then began clearing up the picnic things. 'Enough about this. I don't like to talk about it.'

'About what—Bryant Enterprises? Your family? Your life?' She heard the sharp edge to her own voice and realised that somehow they'd started arguing.

Aaron shot her a narrow glance. 'I told you I didn't know how much I had to give, Zoe.'

She felt her inside freeze, like he'd tipped a bucket of ice water straight into her soul. 'And, less than one day in, you're already tapped out?'

'I don't know.' He pressed his fists against his eyes, his expression one of almost physical pain. 'Damn it, I don't *know*.'

She'd done it again, Zoe thought. Pushed and pushed for more, because she didn't know how to stop. Because she couldn't let things take their natural course. This was day one, for heaven's sake. She could have been a little more patient.

Gently she reached over, put her hands over his and drew them down from his face. 'I'm sorry, Aaron.'

'Sorry?'

'For pushing you into talking about yourself when you're not ready.'

He glanced away. 'I'm sorry I'm not ready.'

'I have this terrible tendency to push,' Zoe confessed with a shaky laugh. 'I should tell you about it right up-front, I suppose.'

'Push?'

'I always ask for more out of a relationship.' She let out another laugh, just as shaky. 'You should see the expression on your face. I know, it's pretty much poison to most commitment-phobes.'

'Are you calling me a commitment-phobe?'

'You and every other man I've dated.'

'And you think it's them—or you?'

'Both.' She hugged her knees to her chest, half amazed that she was admitting this to anyone, much less Aaron. She only hoped he didn't run a mile when he heard about all of her craziness. 'Have you ever been in a high place and had a weird urge to jump off, just because you could? Like in a tower or on a mountain or something?'

Aaron's mouth quirked in a small, surprised smile. 'Umm…sort of.'

'Apparently it's fairly common. Well, I have that urge when it comes to relationships.'

'To jump?'

'Exactly.' She sighed, knowing she needed to explain everything. Even Tim. 'I've had four serious relationships, which at my age may not seem that many, but in some ways it was four too many.'

'How so?'

'I flung myself into each one without really thinking things through, wondering if the guy I was with was right for me, or even right at all. Honourable.'

'Honourable?' Aaron frowned, the effect quite ferocious. 'What kind of guys did you date, Zoe?'

'Jerks, mainly, but I convinced myself I loved each and every one of them. Maybe I really did love them. I'm not sure I know the difference.'

'I can't help you with that one,' Aaron said quietly and she felt her heart twist because, really, what was she doing here with a man who had already told her he would never love her? That he couldn't?

'I rushed into each relationship, determined to make it work. And of course it didn't.'

'Of course? Is it so obvious?'

'Well, Millie always joked that I picked the absolute biggest commitment-phobic toe-rags to date, and she's probably right. I think I actually did it on purpose, on a subconscious level at least. If the guy wasn't that good to begin with, it wasn't my fault if it didn't work out.' She paused, took a breath. 'That part's probably because of Tim.'

Aaron stilled, as if he sensed the importance of that confession. 'Tim?'

'My fiancé.'

He didn't move, his expression didn't even change, but Zoe still felt his shock. 'You were engaged?'

'For about two weeks.' She smiled ruefully, although even now, three years later, the memories still hurt. 'We dated for a year before that, though.'

'What happened?'

'He dumped me.' She tried for insouciance and knew she didn't quite manage it. 'Because his boss told him to.'

'What?'

'Yeah, I know, right? In the twenty-first century and everything.' She shook her head. 'Tim was in finance, some kind of investment thing.'

'Hedge-fund manager?' Aaron guessed with a ghost of a smile and Zoe laughed.

'No, but same ball park. To tell you the truth, I never quite got what he did. That was probably part of the problem.'

'So what problem did his boss have with you?'

'I wasn't right for Tim's image. He was going places, you see, within the firm. Lots of international travel, hosting dinners, that sort of thing. I didn't quite fit in that picture.'

'And so this Tim listened to his boss?'

'Pretty much.'

'He sounds like a total waste of space.'

'Well, I loved him—or at least I thought I did.' Yet she knew that what she felt for Aaron was even more than she'd ever felt for her former fiancé. How scary was that?' 'Anyway,' she resumed, 'when he broke it off, I was devastated. I hadn't even told my family yet—I was waiting till we picked out the ring.'

Aaron cocked his head. 'And you never told them, did you?'

Zoe blinked, surprised that he'd guessed. That he knew. 'No, I didn't. Because two days later Millie's husband and daughter died in a car crash, and the last thing anyone needed to hear about was my sorry little drama.'

'And after, later? Did you tell them then?'

Her throat tightened and she shook her head. 'No.'

'And you weren't going to tell anyone about your pregnancy, were you? About what happened?'

'You did that,' Zoe said, an edge entering her voice again. 'When you phoned Millie.'

'I was worried about you and I wanted someone to be with you even if it couldn't be me.' He paused, his eyes dark. 'Are you angry that I called her?'

'No, I'm not angry. How can I be, when I know you just wanted to help?' She sighed, shaking her head. 'I'm just…embarrassed, really. Angry at myself for screwing up everything in my life.' She blinked, nearly brought to tears by the raw admission.

Aaron was silent for a long moment, and then Zoe felt his hand wrap around the back of her neck, warm and strong. 'You're not screwing this up,' he said softly. 'This is something good.'

'Yes,' Zoe whispered, because she knew it was, even though she was still so afraid that it might all go wrong. That she would push too hard and Aaron would walk away. That he wouldn't have enough to give and she'd be left empty-handed and broken-hearted.

'I think you're too hard on yourself,' he whispered as he drew her inexorably closer. 'And I think you don't like admitting weakness or failure to anyone, even the people who love you. I know how that feels.'

'I bet you do.' He laughed softly, his lips a breath away from hers. And then he kissed her.

It was the first time he'd kissed her since that one night, and this was infinitely sweeter and more precious than anything that had happened before.

His lips moved gently over hers, a reassurance that this *was* good. They were good together. Zoe put her hands on his shoulders and then slid her arms around his neck. Her breasts pressed against his chest and the contact was achingly, agonisingly pleasurable. Aaron deepened the kiss.

Gently he pushed her back onto the blanket, his hand sliding along her middle and then up to cup her breast. Zoe pushed back against him, craving the contact, their legs tangled amidst the detritus of their picnic. She could feel his arousal pressing against her, felt his fingers teasing her, sending arrows of pleasure shooting through her. And frustration, too, because she knew this couldn't go anywhere—or at least not as far as her body desperately wanted.

'I feel like a teenager,' she murmured against his mouth. 'You know I'm not cleared for sex yet, right?'

'I know,' Aaron admitted with a groan. 'But I can't resist touching you.' He slid his hand from her breast down to her middle and then to the pulsing warmth between her thighs. 'Okay?' he murmured and she nodded, because it was more than okay. The pressure of his hand against her was exquisite, and as he moved his fingers with knowing and gentle precision she arched against him and gasped out a sudden, intense climax.

'That was quick,' Aaron said, a smile in his voice as he kissed her mouth.

'It was, wasn't it?' Zoe agreed shakily. She felt dazed by her intense and immediate response to him, more than she'd ever experienced with anyone before. It almost scared her, how much she wanted him.

How much she loved him.

No, she couldn't think like that. Not yet—maybe not ever, no matter how much she wanted to. How much she wanted him to think the same way.

With a smile she pushed Aaron onto his back. 'Now your turn,' she said softly, and his eyes widened.

'You don't have to…'

With a throaty, knowing laugh, she skimmed her hand down the length of his erection. 'Oh, yes,' she said. 'I do.'

And then they didn't talk any more, for there was nothing but the giving and receiving of pleasure, until they lay sated—mostly, anyway, Zoe thought wryly—in each other's arms while the sun shone benevolently overhead.

CHAPTER ELEVEN

'I'D SAY THAT physically you're just about a hundred percent now,' Dr Adams said with a smile. 'But tell me how you feel.'

Zoe slid off the examining table. 'I feel a hundred percent,' she said firmly. She'd been back in New York for three days, and the doctor's clean bill of health was music to her ears. At last she could be with Aaron as she wanted to be…as she was desperate to be ever since their precious few weeks on St Julian's.

'Have you considered counselling?' Dr Adams asked. 'Or therapy? The experience you had was traumatic, and there will be ongoing—'

'I know that.' She nodded, although she really didn't want to talk about that now. 'I work in therapy myself, so I understand that and I'm looking into it. I know it will take a long time to heal emotionally.'

'We have resources, if you need them. A support group meets here at the hospital.'

'Thank you,' Zoe said. 'I'll look into it.'

As she left the hospital she had a spring in her step—and a fear in her heart. As pleased as she was about the doctor's all-clear, she couldn't help but feel nervous for what lay ahead. The last few weeks with Aaron had been wonderful…but it hadn't been easy.

They'd spent two weeks on St Julian's, which Zoe knew was an enormous amount of time for Aaron to be away from his work. He'd checked his phone and email often, and spent most afternoons tele-commuting while she'd lounged by the pool. But even with the constant pressures of work, there had been times—wonderful times—with just the two of them. Walks along the beach and candlelit dinners; long nights wrapped in each other's arms and endless kisses and touching that just didn't go quite far enough.

It had all been wonderful, but at the same time Zoe still sensed a distance in Aaron, a place he didn't allow her—or anyone—access. In exasperation she'd once asked sarcastically, 'Do you have any *hobbies*?'

To which he'd replied flatly, 'No.'

The man was a machine. A machine who still didn't want to be known or understood, at least not completely. How could a relationship survive in those kinds of conditions?

Millie had told her to give it time. Upon returning to New York, Zoe had moved in with Millie and Chase rather than go back to her lonely apartment. She wasn't ready to move back in with Aaron—not that he'd even offered.

The night she'd got back Chase had made himself scarce; Millie had made margaritas and nachos—their snack of choice—and they'd both curled up on the sofa and had the kind of heart-to-heart they hadn't had in years.

'I'd be the first one to say I wasn't sure about Aaron,' Millie said bluntly. 'About you and Aaron. From what Chase has told me, the guy seemed like a complete jerk—arrogant, autocratic, totally controlling.'

'But?' Zoe said, trying to smile. She knew there was a different man underneath that authoritative facade, but she didn't know if she could trust him—or if that man could love her.

'He clearly cares about you. And he obviously has wanted to do the right thing for you.'

'And the baby?' Zoe filled in. 'That hardly counts now. And doing the right thing isn't a foundation for a relationship.'

'No,' Millie answered. 'But it shows the nature of his character. He's honourable, Zoe. He's good.'

'That only goes so far.' Zoe swallowed, her fears seeming to crowd her throat, making it hard to speak. 'Anyway, maybe he just wanted to do the right thing because he felt guilty.'

Millie frowned. 'You've said that before. What did he have to feel guilty about?'

Zoe hesitated, then decided she needed someone to confide in completely. 'When I first told him I was pregnant, he offered me fifty thousand dollars to have an abortion.'

Millie was silent for a long moment. 'I guess he changed his mind,' she finally said.

'I probably shouldn't have even told you. He regretted it, and he said it was a bad decision. But—'

'It's hard to forget.'

She nodded. 'I can't help but think that it's part of who he is—to leap to that conclusion, to even want that. And, even though he's shown he's different with me, he *can* be different, I'm not sure if that's enough. If he can be different enough. Who's the real man—the one who made that offer, or the one who said it was a mistake?'

'You need to give him time. People don't change overnight.'

'I know that. And I'm trying not to push but—I'm scared. I don't want to be hurt again, and worse this time, because I care more for Aaron than anyone else—even Tim.'

Millie frowned. 'Even Tim?'

Zoe thought of what Aaron had said: *I think you don't like admitting weakness or failure to anyone, even the people who love you.* He was right, she knew; he was right because he was the same. *I know how that feels.* 'I never told you about Tim,' she said, and then slowly she began to tell the story of her ex-fiancé.

'I wish you'd told me when it happened,' Millie said when Zoe had finished. 'I know the timing was bad, but still…'

'I didn't tell anyone.'

'There's something I never told you,' Millie said quietly. 'About Rob.'

'Rob?' Millie didn't talk much about her former husband; as far as Zoe had ever known, they'd had a great relationship.

'When I was pregnant with Charlotte, he wanted me to have an abortion.'

Zoe's mouth dropped open. 'So you know how that feels.'

'It wasn't the right time, he felt. We still had so

much to prove in our careers. I almost went along with him.' She was silent for a long moment. 'I even made an appointment. I walked out of it at the last minute—I still feel guilty about it sometimes.'

'Oh, Mills.' Zoe shook her head. 'Aaron told me I was too hard on myself, and I think you are, too.'

'That's what Chase says,' Millie admitted with a small smile.

'Those Bryant brothers. They know what they're talking about.'

Millie leaned forward, her face turning serious. 'Do you love him, Zoe?'

Zoe swallowed, the question reverberating inside her, as well as its undeniable answer. 'I'm afraid I do.'

Now as she walked towards the subway to go to her art-therapy session, she wondered why she'd said it like that: *I'm afraid I do.*

Was love that scary? Yes, it most certainly was. It was terrifying…especially when Aaron had made no promises. He'd already told her he didn't know how much he had to give, that he wasn't even sure he could love. When there had been a baby to consider, Zoe had thought she could accept those conditions.

But now…now she knew she'd been fooling herself. Those conditions were terrible, and she could never accept them. Never live with them, day after endless day. Maybe she'd convinced herself before that she could because part of her had already been falling for him, was already desperate.

But now, for once, she wanted to be strong. She didn't want to make the same mistake over and over again—falling for a guy who was all wrong for her, who would never love her back, and this time so much harder.

If I was stronger, I would end it now.

Give it time.

Yet how much time? How much possibility for pain? She took a deep breath, let it out slowly. She had no answer to those questions.

Aaron drummed his fingers against his thigh as his limo sped towards Millie and Chase's town-house on Central Park West, where he was picking up Zoe for an evening out.

He felt as if there were bands of steel wrapped around his skull, tightening with every second. The two weeks he'd spent on St Julian's had been costly, perhaps more costly than he'd ever know. Someone was continuing to make a move on Bryant Enterprises, buying up shares, skulking in the background. Meanwhile the uncertain economy in Europe and Asia was wreaking havoc on the funds Aaron managed. He felt as if he were teetering on a precipice of disaster, and his only salvation was Zoe.

Had his father felt like this, with his legion of mistresses? Had he only been able to find peace and even sanity with the women who had controlled and ultimately ruined him?

And would Aaron be the same?

During the last weeks with Zoe, he'd fought against that fear. His father had led his business, his family and even his life into disaster because of his attachment to women—and one woman in particular. When Aaron had discovered his father's weakness, he'd vowed not to share it. Not to give anyone control over him, not to need anyone that much, and certainly not to love.

Yet Zoe was breaking through all those boundaries, breaking him. He needed her, maybe even loved her.

No.

The denial was instinctive, necessary. It was how he'd lived his life. Could he really change that much? Did he even want to?

The limo pulled up in front of Chase and Millie's brownstone. 'I'll just be a minute,' Aaron said tersely, and with his mind still in a ferment he went to fetch Zoe.

She was still getting ready upstairs when Aaron arrived and he spent a few awkward moments with Chase, conscious now of Zoe's question: *Why aren't you close with your brothers?*

He never had been, even as a child. He'd been set apart from an early age, too early for him actually to remember. He was the oldest, the most responsible, the one who had to be in charge. And when his father had died and he'd realised just what that meant, what it would cost, that had driven him and his brothers even further apart.

Now Chase smiled easily and cracked open a beer. 'How's it going?'

'Fine,' Aaron said tersely. He could not relax. Not with Chase, and perhaps not even with Zoe. He felt the pressure build inside his head, inside his heart. He wanted her, needed her—and that terrified him.

Chase arched an eyebrow. 'You sure about that?'

'I'm sure, Chase.'

'Everything's good with BE?'

Aaron's mouth twisted. He did not want to talk about Bryant Enterprises with Chase, or with any-

one. He did not even want to think about it. 'Everything's fine, Chase.'

Chase shrugged and nodded. 'And you'd tell me
if it wasn't.'

No, of course he wouldn't. 'What is this?' Aaron
arched an eyebrow sardonically. 'It's not like we've
had heart-to-hearts in the past, Chase.'

'Always a good time to start.'

Aaron shook his head. 'I have nothing to say. I'm
fine. Bryant Enterprises is fine.' He felt his throat
constrict and silently cursed. What was *wrong* with
him? Zoe was making him weak, needy. Desperate. 'Damn it, everything's fine,' he said hoarsely,
and turned away.

Chase, thankfully, didn't reply, and a few minutes later Zoe came downstairs. Aaron viewed her
as if through a haze; he felt his temples throb and
the pressure inside him intensify. Yet still he could
acknowledge how beautiful she looked: her hair
was swept to one side with a sparkly clip and she
wore an off-the-shoulder gown in a deep blue that
made her eyes shine. She smiled as she came down
the stairs, but dimly he registered there was something tentative about her smile, something almost
wary. Then he realised he was scowling.

Damn. Already this evening felt like it was

going wrong. Somehow he forced the corners of his mouth up into a smile. 'You look beautiful.'

'Thank you.' She still looked uncertain but as Millie joined Chase in the foyer Zoe lifted her chin and took his arm. With a nod to his brother and sister-in-law, Aaron stepped out into the night.

Zoe could feel the tension in Aaron's body, his arm like a steel bar under her hand. She waited until they were in the limo, speeding downtown towards the exclusive club where Aaron had been invited for a cocktail party, to ask the question that hammered inside her heart.

'What's wrong?'

'Nothing.'

'Aaron.' She turned to him, tried to make out his expression in the shadowy darkness of the car. Streetlights washed his face in pale yellow every few seconds. She saw how tight-lipped and hard-eyed he looked, and felt her heart quail. Surely it—they—weren't starting to unravel already. Yet, looking at Aaron's hard profile, she felt as if they were. 'Something's obviously wrong,' she said quietly. 'And if you don't want to talk about it, just say so.'

'Fine,' Aaron answered tersely. 'I don't want to talk about it.'

Well, she'd asked for that one. Zoe felt her nails dig into her palms. 'Fine,' she said, trying to sound calm, but a petulant note crept into her voice and she turned to the window.

Don't overreact, she told herself. *Don't assume it's just like every time before. Give it time, like Millie said.* Yet she desperately craved reassurance, for Aaron to say anything that would bridge the chasm that was widening between them. He didn't speak.

'I went to the doctor today,' she said after a few minutes when they'd been stuck at a traffic light on Park Avenue for a while. Aaron turned to her.

'Is everything okay?'

'Yes.' She took a breath, plunged. 'I've been given the all-clear.' She waited and Aaron just stared. 'You know.'

'I know?' he asked, and to her amazement she thought she heard a teasing note in his voice. She felt a tidal wave of relief crash over her.

'Don't you?' she teased back, and in the wash of the streetlights she saw Aaron's smile.

'I hope I do.' She felt his hand on her shoulder, then stealing around her neck. He drew her to him and kissed her softly on the lips. 'Tonight?' he whispered. 'If you're ready?'

Dear lord, she was more than ready. Even if she was still scared and uncertain and so desperately wanted this to *work*. Her mouth still brushing his, she nodded.

Zoe thought she would enjoy the party more than she did: champagne and fancy appetisers; amusing and glamorous people; and, best of all, Aaron by her side, his hand on her elbow, his body so tantalisingly near...which was why she could hardly wait to leave.

All she could think about was what would happen after the party. She imagined them riding home in Aaron's limo; going up the lift to his penthouse, and stepping into that darkened penthouse, the lights of Manhattan spread all around them in a glittering map.

And then...

'So you're a therapist?'

Zoe jerked her mind back to the conversation she'd been having with several socialites. 'An art therapist.'

'I didn't know there was such a thing.'

Briefly she described her work, sensing their scepticism, and then to her surprise Aaron jumped in. 'It's especially effective with children. They're much more likely to be able to communicate their feelings through pictures than words.'

Zoe stared at him in surprise while the two glamorous women nodded. 'I guess that makes sense.'

Only because a gorgeous billionaire had told them, she thought cynically. When she and Aaron were alone, sipping champagne, she gave him a teasing look over the rim of her crystal flute. 'You sounded pretty certain back there.'

He shrugged. 'I guess I'm converted.'

She gave a little laugh. 'Really? How?'

'You're very passionate about what you do and believe. I admire that.'

'Passionate,' Zoe repeated, and saw Aaron's eyes flare with heat.

'Passionate,' he agreed huskily. 'Now, how about we get out of here?'

She could only nod. Her heart had started thudding and her palms were slick. Now it would happen. *Finally.*

Aaron took their glasses and deposited them on a waiter's tray. Then he was taking her by the elbow and whisking her out of the party into the crisp autumn night. The limo was waiting as always, and as Zoe slid in she felt her first attack of nerves.

Stupid, maybe, when they'd already slept together. This wasn't the first time.

Yet it felt like the first time, because it was so different now. At least, she wanted it to be different. She wanted it to feel like more, to mean more.

Yet she was still afraid it might not.

'You look nervous,' Aaron said and took her hand.

Zoe tried to smile. 'I am,' she admitted. 'Maybe I shouldn't be, but—'

'I'm a bit nervous, too.'

Zoe let out a shocked laugh. She could hardly believe Aaron could ever be nervous about anything. He certainly looked relaxed sitting there, his legs stretched out, one arm resting on the seat above her head. 'You are not,' she said.

'Well, I must admit anticipation trumps any nervousness. I feel like I've been waiting a long time for this.'

'So do I,' she whispered.

They didn't speak again as they arrived at his building, and just as she'd imagined they rode up in the lift in a silence that was tense with expectation. Zoe could feel her heart beating so hard she wondered if Aaron could hear its thud, or see the pounding underneath the thin silk of her evening gown.

The doors swooshed open; Aaron took her by the hand and led her into the darkened apartment. Her dress whispered against her bare legs as he drew her to him, his hands framing her face in a way that was so achingly tender, infinitely gentle.

He kissed her once, softly, barely a brush of his lips against hers. Zoe sighed in surrender.

And then his phone buzzed in his pocket.

It almost seemed like a joke. It was certainly fitting, considering the nature of their first meeting. She felt Aaron tense, felt his hand leave her face and reach for his pocket.

'Aaron,' she said desperately, because she had a terrible instinct that if he took that call their night would be over. And maybe she should be understanding; he had a high-pressured job and this was, after all, only one night.

But it was an important night, a defining moment, and Zoe felt all her uncertainties and fears rise up in her as she put her hand over Aaron's, trapping it before he could reach his phone.

'Don't.'

'Zoe, it could be important—'

'Could be,' she repeated, her fingers twining

with his. 'And this is important, Aaron, isn't it? What's happening between us?'

His voice was low and rough with want. 'Of course it is.'

'Then please, just leave it for a few hours. Surely it can wait?'

'And you can't?' He spoke tonelessly, but she knew what he was asking her. Was she giving him an ultimatum?

Zoe hesitated. She didn't want to be demanding; she wanted to make this work. But neither was she willing to accept what little Aaron had to give, or set a precedent where everything but her came first.

'No,' she said finally. 'I can't.'

Aaron hesitated. Zoe held her breath. Had she just made a huge mistake? Had she ruined everything already by pushing yet again? And yet it had been necessary…hadn't it?

The phone buzzed again.

After a tense and endless moment Aaron removed his hand from hers. He took his phone out of his pocket and without looking at it tossed it onto a chair. 'There.'

'Thank you,' Zoe said, and she stood on her tiptoes to kiss him, another brush of the lips, but

Aaron took it and made it his own, deepening it so his tongue thrust into her mouth and Zoe felt as if her soul had been set on fire.

There was a raw urgency to Aaron's kiss, to his hands, as he unzipped her dress and slid it from her shoulders. He kissed her mouth, her throat, and then moved lower to kiss her breasts, slipping aside the scrappy lace of her bra.

Zoe gasped at the feel of his mouth, so cool and hard, hot and soft all at once, on her bare flesh. She rested her hands on his shoulders to steady herself as he moved lower, slipping the dress down her hips and legs, his mouth following a blazing trail.

'Aaron…'

'I need you, Zoe. I need you so much.' The words were raw, a guttural confession that Zoe knew Aaron meant—even if he didn't want to. And, while need wasn't love, it was something. It was a start.

She kicked the dress away from her high-heel-shod feet as Aaron sank to her knees in front of her. She swayed where she stood as her hands clenched around his shoulders and his mouth found the hot, pulsing centre of her.

'Aaron…' she said again, amazed at how quickly he could bring her to that precipice of pleasure. Already she felt the first waves of her climax crashing over her, and she was helpless to stop it. Her knees buckled as she cried out and Aaron swept his arm under her legs, carrying her easily to the bedroom.

His eyes were dark, his face almost savage with intent desire as he stripped off his tuxedo so he was gloriously naked, all hard, taut muscle and sleek skin. Zoe reached for him.

The press of his naked body against hers had her gasping aloud from the sheer, intense joy of it, and as he kissed her, his hands moving over her body, his fingers finding her secret, sensitive places, Zoe found her body straining towards another climax.

'You're going to kill me,' she gasped and he laughed low in his throat as his fingers slid inside her.

'It would be a good way to go.'

'Yes, it would,' she agreed, and with a superhuman effort—because what he was doing felt so amazingly good—she slipped out from under him and pushed him onto his back. 'But this isn't a one-man show, you know.'

'No?'

'No.'

And then it was her turn to explore him, every kiss and caress evoking a shuddering response that had her thrilling with seductive power—and a far greater emotion. *Love.*

She loved him. She'd been fighting against it, lecturing herself not to, and yet here it was, pure, simple and so very right. The doubts fell away and as Aaron finally rolled her over and entered her in one pure stroke, Zoe felt tears come to her eyes.

Just as before his gaze locked with hers and she felt the moment of raw need stretch and grow into something greater, something more powerful than pleasure.

'I love you,' she whispered and Aaron tensed above her, his face a mask, but Zoe didn't care. She felt, in that moment, that her love would be enough. She put her arms around him and arched upwards as he drove into her again, filling her up into completion. 'I love you,' she said again, and Aaron didn't answer.

He buried his face in her neck as he moved inside her, and then Zoe couldn't think or worry about his silence because she was swept away on a tide of pleasure too great to resist, too wonderful to worry about anything else.

* * *

Aaron lay in his bed, his arm around Zoe's shoulders, his heart thundering in his chest.

I love you.

The words had humbled him, felled him, because no one had ever said them to him before. Not his father, who had lectured him about responsibility and duty; not his mother, who had been too wrapped up in her own misery. Not a woman, for the women he'd been with before, if they'd deluded themselves that they cared about him at all, would certainly have known better than to say as much.

But Zoe was different. And he was different with Zoe, because when she'd said those three words he'd wanted to hear them. He'd received them with a kind of dazed joy, even if he wasn't sure if he could say them back. He still didn't know if he had that depth of emotion in him.

'You don't have to say anything,' Zoe said quietly, and although she sounded calm he still heard a faint thread of hurt in her voice. Of course she was hurt. Generally, when a woman said 'I love you', the man was supposed to say something—'I love you, too' being the preferred option. He knew that much at least.

'I'm glad you love me,' he said, pulling her close, and she let out a little laugh.

'Well, that's something.'

'I'm glad you think so.'

She rolled over, her hair brushing his bare chest as she kissed him. 'You're glad about a lot of things, aren't you?'

'Yes, I am.'

She smiled softly and from the other room Aaron heard a sound that had him tensing, a sound he'd blanked out in the last hour. His phone.

He needed to answer it. Part of him wanted to ignore it, wanted to stay in the safe and warm cocoon of Zoe's embrace, but he knew how much unrest there had been in both the economy and Bryant Enterprises. He needed to check his messages.

'Just a minute,' he said, and slid from the bed.

Zoe propped herself up one elbow. 'You're going to check your phone, aren't you?'

'It's been an hour.'

'I didn't realise you'd set a timer. Or is it just your internal clock?' She sounded waspish, and Aaron felt the first flicker of anger.

'Be reasonable. It could be something important.'

'Fine.' She rolled over, her back to him, and with

an impatient shrug Aaron slid on his boxer shorts and stalked to the living room.

He reached for his phone, his heart seeming to freeze within him as he saw how many messages he'd missed. He listened to the first voicemail with a numbing sense of disbelief.

'Aaron, there's been an emergency meeting of the board of trustees. Apparently, it's allowable when there is a majority shareholder...'

The mystery man who was trying to buy up his company. He listened to the next message, and then the next, as his second-in-command detailed the events of the meeting.

And then the verdict—stark, impossible: 'You've been voted down as CEO.'

He'd lost Bryant Enterprises. And all because of a woman.

CHAPTER TWELVE

ZOE LAY IN bed, her body still tingling from Aaron's love-making even as she berated herself for being so bitchy about him taking his messages. Honestly, would she ever learn anything from her past relationships? It was just that she was so desperate and afraid. Neither were admirable qualities, and certainly not ones she wanted to possess in any relationship—especially not this one, the most important of all. She hated feeling like the person who gave more, who needed more, who cared more. Who loved.

She'd told Aaron it didn't matter if he didn't love her, but she knew it did. Of course it did. If he loved her, she'd hand him his stupid phone herself. She'd understand, she wouldn't care about such trivial moments. It was because she knew he didn't that those little moments became far too important. Defining.

Sighing, she stared up at the ceiling. Only moments ago she'd felt so joyously certain, yet now the doubts crept right back in. She took a deep breath and forced herself to stay calm. She'd be honest with Aaron. She'd apologise to him for being stupid about the phone. She'd tell him what she needed.

It seemed like a good plan and Zoe had sat up in bed, the sheet wrapped around her, when Aaron strode into the bedroom, his face as frighteningly blank as it had ever been.

Still, she had to try.

'Aaron, I'm sorry I was obnoxious about you checking your phone. I know it's such a small thing, and I clearly overreacted.' Aaron didn't answer. He sat on the edge of the bed, his back to her. 'Aaron?' she asked uncertainly. 'Is something wrong?'

'Is something wrong?' he repeated tonelessly. 'You could say that.'

A cold, creeping fear took hold of her heart. 'Was it the phone? Was there a message—?'

'There were twenty-two messages.' Aaron cut her off, his voice still flat.

'Oh.' She hugged her knees to her chest. 'I guess it was something important.'

'You guessed right.' Aaron raked his hands

through his hair, his body in the grip of some terrible emotion. Then he dropped his hands and Zoe had the horrible feeling that he'd just come to some major decision—and one she didn't want to hear.

He scooped her dress off the floor and tossed it to her. Zoe caught it instinctively, the sheet slipping from her breasts. 'You should go.'

'*Go?*'

'This isn't working. It never could have worked. Everything between us has been a mistake.'

It was as if he were saying every fear her heart had whispered, turning them into terrible realities. 'You don't mean that, Aaron.'

He turned to her, his eyes hard and cold. 'I mean it absolutely.'

'You're just going to end it like this? Kick me out?'

'A clean break is better.'

She shook her head slowly, still numb with disbelief. Ten minutes ago he'd been inside her. 'Who the hell was on that phone?' she asked and Aaron didn't answer; he just gathered her underwear and shoes and deposited them on the bed.

'I'll have my limo drive you to Millie and Chase's,' he said, and left the room.

Zoe sat frozen in the bed they'd just shared, her

crumpled dress between her clenched fingers. Her mind spun uselessly, for she had no idea what had just happened…or why. Had a single phone call really made such a difference, or had Aaron been stringing her along the whole while? In either case, she had judged badly—again. And now she was left reeling and hurting more than ever before.

She dressed quickly, feeling sordid and shamed as she put on her crumpled evening gown. She slipped on her heels and did as much repair as she could to her face and hair. Then she took a deep breath and headed for the living room and Aaron.

She didn't know what to expect, but when she emerged from the bedroom he didn't even look at her. He'd dressed in a business suit, which seemed odd at this time of night. It had to be nearing midnight.

She walked to the lift doors and still he didn't say anything. In stunned disbelief she realised he was just going to let her walk out of his life for ever. In fact, that was what he seemed to want.

Emotions tightened in her chest and clogged her throat. 'I think,' she managed after a moment when he still hadn't so much as turned his head, 'I deserve an explanation at least.'

'There's no point.'

'Really?' Her voice choked and she strived to even it—then wondered why she wanted to hide how much he'd hurt her. Devastated her. 'And how did you come to that conclusion?'

Finally he looked at her and then Zoe wished he hadn't. He was the same man she'd first met at Millie's wedding, cold and pitiless, arrogant and hard. A man she hadn't liked or respected. Was that the real Aaron, and the rest had been no more than a facade? 'It doesn't matter, Zoe,' he said flatly, and he sounded impatient, as if he could barely stand to give her these few seconds of his time. 'All that matters is that this—us—was a mistake.'

'A mistake.'

'Yes.'

She stared at him, searching for some crack in the mask, some sign that he still was the man she wanted and loved underneath. There was nothing. Even so, a part of her longed to try to reach him, to cross the frozen silence between them, take his face in her hands and kiss his lips. To insist that she knew him now and he wasn't this man. He was someone kind, tender and good. He was the man she loved.

The words were there, clogged in her throat, on her lips. A flicker of impatience crossed Aaron's face like a shadow, and with it came Zoe's defeat. She'd done this before—tried and begged and believed when she shouldn't have. When Tim had ended it, she'd insisted she could change for him, that it could work. She'd begged him not to give up on her. The memory now was unbearably shaming; long ago Zoe had promised herself she would never debase herself so again. Then she'd gone on basically to do the same thing in three other relationships.

She wouldn't do it now.

Lifting her chin, she met Aaron's gaze straight on. 'Goodbye, Aaron,' she said with as much dignity as she could muster. He didn't answer, and as the lift doors opened and she stepped inside she couldn't keep from some of the awful hurt spilling out. 'I hope you go to hell,' she spat, the words ending on a sob, and the doors closed on his stony, unchanging expression.

Two days later Aaron sat in his former office and stared at the remnants of his life. A few boxes of confidential files were pretty much all he had. There were no photos, no mementoes, no personal items beyond a spare suit to remove from the executive office of Bryant Enterprises. The high-rise office building in midtown had been in the Bryant family since it had been built back in the 1930s.

Now it belonged to someone else, some techno-wizard from California who had masterminded the hostile takeover of his company. Today was Aaron's last day.

The newspapers' business pages had been full of his failure: *Bryant Enterprises Crumbles!* And *No More Bryant in BE* He'd read every article, punishing himself even as he refused to give into the pulsing pain that coursed through him unre-lentingly. He would not succumb to self-pity. How could he, when this was all his fault?

He knew it wasn't the simple matter of not taking a phone call. He wasn't so paranoid as to believe the course of his fortune had changed overnight. No, it had happened long before that; it had started at Millie and Chase's wedding when Zoe Parker had taken his phone and he'd let her. He could have got it back sooner. He could have handled that whole situation differently, but instead he'd given her control because he'd been so in lust with her right from the beginning. Enthralled and excited by her daring, by her playful smile and the spark he'd seen in her eyes.

And from that moment on he'd lost his focus—

asking her to move in with him, coming home early because she'd asked him to, spending two *weeks* on a remote Caribbean island. All of it added up to a perfect opportunity for someone to step in and sweep away all his work like so many flimsy dominoes. And he'd allowed it to happen.

Enough. Aaron rose from the desk. Self-recrimination was almost as bad as self-pity and a waste of time. What was done was done. He was hardly destitute; he'd received a substantial pay-out and St Julian's, owned jointly by all three brothers, remained in the family. His apartment was his own, without a mortgage, as was a summer house he owned in the Catskills. He had some personal investments. Everything else was gone.

He'd practically given it away.

Shaking his head, Aaron reached for his coat and the briefcase he wouldn't need any more. He'd have one of the errand boys bring down his boxes. He'd have to take a cab; the limo was a corporate perk.

'Hello, Aaron.'

Aaron jerked his head around to see, to his surprise, his brother Luke standing in the doorway. 'Come to gloat?' he asked, hearing the bitterness mixed with gallows humour in his voice. 'I suppose I deserve it.'

'I'm not gloating.'

'I know I never gave you the control you wanted.' For fifteen years Luke had worked for Bryant's retail arm, but Aaron had still initialled every decision. It had been a deliberate choice, because from the beginning everything had felt so perilous. Losing control would have meant losing the company...just as he'd done now.

'It's true you didn't,' Luke said, stepping into the office. 'Why didn't you, as a matter of interest?'

'What do you mean?'

'I always thought it was just because you were a control freak. Or that you didn't trust me.'

'I didn't trust you,' Aaron answered bluntly, and Luke let out a short laugh.

'So it really was that simple.'

No, nothing had been simple since his father had died and he'd discovered the empire he'd inherited was rotten to the core. He'd never felt so betrayed in that moment, abandoned by his idol, alone at twenty-one to resurrect a business bankrupted by his father's folly. And he'd succeeded...for a while. Until his own foolishness had cost him everything.

'I didn't trust anyone,' Aaron said. 'Not even myself. And I was right, wasn't I?' He let out a bitter laugh. 'I lost everything.'

Luke was silent for a long moment. 'And don't you think that was a choice?'

'A choice?' A bad one, then, to follow his libido rather than his brain. His heart rather than his head.

'Aaron, I know you're piling the guilt on yourself now, but you are one hell of a sharp guy. I don't think an upstart computer geek could steal your company from under your nose without you knowing about it.'

Aaron stilled, his gaze narrowing in on his brother. 'What are you saying?'

'I'm no shrink, but I'm saying that some part of you knew this was happening—and allowed it.'

'No.' The denial was immediate, instinctive.

'Father always put far too many expectations on you, even when you were a little kid. I think you knew you were going to be CEO when you were about six. Is it any wonder you might want to rebel against that?'

Aaron didn't answer. His mind was spinning with this new knowledge, this sudden realisation that Luke was right—that he'd known about the possible takeover for weeks, maybe even months, and had in some secret part of himself wanted it to happen. Had wanted to lose Bryant Enterprises because for once he wanted to be his own man, free to chose his own path.

A path that would have included Zoe…if in the first shock of loss and fear he hadn't pushed her away and destroyed any chance they had together.

'How do you feel now?' Luke asked quietly. 'Now that it's all gone, and none of it matters anymore?'

Aaron considered the question. He'd been numb since it all started unravelling three days ago, getting through the mechanics of each day, of taking a life apart. And now? 'I feel…free,' he admitted in a kind of hesitant wonder, and then he looked away. The confession felt like a betrayal.

'That's how I felt too,' Luke said. 'When I walked away from Bryant Enterprises. I didn't realise what a shackle it had been until it was gone.'

A shackle. Yes, it had chained him, maimed him: the endless attempts to rebuild a company teetering on the edge of disaster; all his beliefs about his father; his family destroyed.

'Bryant Enterprises has been in our family for a hundred years,' he said in a raw voice. 'You can't just walk away from that.'

'That was the problem, wasn't it?' Luke answered, his mouth twisting sardonically. 'It was damn hard for me to walk away. I can only imagine how difficult it's been for you.'

'Even so.'

'That company was killing you, Aaron. Maybe you can't see it, but I can from here.'

Aaron blinked hard. He knew Luke was right, even if he hated to admit it. Even if his freedom felt like weakness. 'Still,' he said with a ragged sigh, 'I made a huge mess of things.'

Luke remained silent for a moment. 'You mean Zoe.'

'How do you know?'

'I don't, really. Chase told me a little. Do you love her?'

Yes. The admission, made in the silence of his own heart, stunned him. He knew it was true. And it was too damn late. 'It doesn't matter.'

'How can you say that?'

'Because she won't forgive me,' Aaron snapped. 'Even if I wanted to be forgiven.'

'And you don't?'

Did he want to go back to Zoe a defeated, ruined man? No. He wanted to return to her on his terms—proud, in control. Arrogant. Autocratic. A control freak, just as she'd once called him.

Was he capable of change? Was he capable of

going to Zoe and admitting his weaknesses, his failures? The thought was abhorrent…yet necessary.

Perhaps this was the only way. He gave his brother a wry smile. 'This is tough.'

Luke let out a laugh and shook his head. 'Don't I know it.'

'You're happy, though, with Aurelie,' Aaron said, and he nodded.

'Absolutely. And you can be too, Aaron, but you're right, it's not easy. That doesn't mean it's not worth it.'

As he left the building for the last time Aaron felt that shackle finally slip off. Strange, how liberating it truly was. He had no idea what he'd do now, but the realisation that Bryant Enterprises was no longer his responsibility, his burden, almost made him giddy with relief…instantly followed by an instinctive disgust.

What kind of man did that make him?

A free man, a man at liberty to make his own choice. Zoe had been right when she'd asked if it was the lack of choice he'd minded. Now he'd made his choice, even if he hadn't realised it at the time. He'd chosen freedom, independence. Possibility.

Shaking his head, Aaron knew it would be a long time before he could reconcile his conflicting emotions. Before he could be at peace with what had happened.

And as for what had happened with Zoe…regret lanced through him. He'd treated her so very badly, hadn't even been willing to give her an explanation, a chance. He'd been reacting on instinct, out of fear. And not just fear, but disgust; thinking he had acted just like his father. Been as weak as the man he'd once idolised.

He'd been wrong.

Would Zoe give him another chance? He felt his heart thud at the thought of confronting her, asking for her forgiveness. He'd been able to say a few careless sorries to her before, but this was something entirely new and different, and all too risky.

And yet necessary.

He hailed a cab and told him to head uptown, to Millie and Chase's brownstone.

Millie answered the door when he arrived, her face pulling into a ferocious frown.

'I should slam this door in your face.'

'Is Zoe here?'

'If she were, I wouldn't—'

'Millie, please.' He held up one hand to stem her tirade, and she sighed.

'The only reason I'm *not* slamming this door in your face is because I happen to know that Bryant men can be rather stupid about women and love.'

'Phenomenally stupid.'

'That was the right answer.' Millie smiled, but it quickly faded. 'Don't hurt her, Aaron. She's been hurt before. I didn't even know how badly.'

'I know.'

'She told you?'

He nodded. She'd been honest with him. She'd been vulnerable. And he hadn't, not really. Now was his chance—and it frightened the hell out of him. 'Where is she?' he asked, and Millie told him.

Zoe smiled at Robert, the little boy who had been coming to the community centre for several months now.

Today he had made some encouraging strides; he'd drawn a picture of his family, including his father, taking care with the minute details: the sun shining, the smiles on their faces, the buttons on their shirts. Then he'd stared at it for a long moment and said quietly, 'I wish it was like that.'

Zoe's heart had contracted inside her and she laid

a hand on Robert's shoulder. *I wish it was like that too, Robert,* she thought. At least acceptance was part of the grieving process, and both she and the little boy were grieving.

Now Robert had gone and Zoe was just clearing up the art supplies scattered across the table. The centre would be closing in a little while. She felt someone watching her and, stiffening slightly because the centre's doors were open to whomever chose to walk inside, she turned to glance at the doorway to the art room…and stopped in shock when she saw it was Aaron.

She should have nothing to say to him, she told herself numbly as he came forward. She shouldn't even acknowledge his presence, not after the way he'd treated her. She turned back to the table and scooped up a handful of crayons, her fingers shaking, and dropped several.

Aaron reached over and put the dropped ones in the basket. 'Hello, Zoe.' She didn't answer. Couldn't. She concentrated on the crayons and Aaron finally said quietly, 'I'd like to talk to you.'

'There are no words you could say that I want to hear.'

He was silent for a moment and Zoe didn't dare

look at him. 'Perhaps I could draw a picture,' he finally said, and she sat back, folding her arms.

'A little art therapy? It can work wonders.'

'Then let me have a go.' He sat down at the table, looking incongruous in his business suit. Zoe watched as he took a piece of paper and a couple of crayons. As with everything, he worked carefully, diligently, his brow furrowed in concentration as he drew a couple of stick figures.

'Very nice,' she said, sarcasm edging her voice. 'Who are those supposed to be?'

'Me.' He pointed to the sad-faced stick figure in the centre of the picture. 'You.' She was another sad-looking stick figure in the corner of the picture.

'I'd say that's about right.'

He glanced up from the paper. 'I'm no artist, Zoe, but I would like to talk to you. I sincerely regret what happened between us the other night.'

'What happened between us? That suggests shared responsibility, Aaron—and, as I recall, it was all you. I just sat there like a lemon.' Bitterness spiked her words. If she had to have her heart broken, couldn't she have acted a little stronger, a little more in control?

'You're right,' Aaron answered. 'I acted like a

complete bastard and I want to apologise. And explain. Will you please let me?'

She stared at him for a long moment, indecision warring within her. She'd never been in this scenario before; no one had ever come back, wanting to explain or apologise. Part of her wanted to stay strong and another part desperately wanted to hear what he had to say.

'All right,' she said at last. 'But the centre is closing. Let me clear up and we can go outside.'

Aaron helped her put away the art supplies and mop the floor, neither of them speaking beyond the basics, and a few minutes later they stepped out into a beautiful late October afternoon.

They walked in mutual, silent agreement towards Washington Square, the leaves above them crimson and gold.

'So,' Zoe said when they'd reached a park bench. She sat down, her arms folded, legs crossed, her position one of defence. 'What do you have to say?'

'I shouldn't have asked you to leave the other night.'

'*Asked* me to leave?'

'Kicked you out,' Aaron amended. 'That phone call—the one I took—was a voicemail message calling an emergency meeting of my board of trustees.'

She frowned, not really getting it. 'Why?'

'Someone has been secretly buying up shares in Bryant Enterprises for a while now. I've been trying to keep an eye on it, but the other night he called the meeting and basically had me fired.'

She straightened, her mouth nearly dropping open in shock. 'Fired?'

'Basically. He replaced me as CEO. I no longer have a role in Bryant Enterprises, or a majority of the shares.'

'But…' She shook her head, still stunned. Aaron spoke so flatly, without any emotion at all, yet it sounded like everything had been taken away from him. 'What did that have to do with me?' she asked at last. 'Were you just angry?'

'Ashamed,' Aaron corrected quietly. 'But to understand why I need to go back a little further. I told you a bit about my father—how he singled me out from an early age to take over the company. My whole life was oriented towards that—every exchange, every conversation was a lesson in duty and responsibility. I had to be tough, above petty things like relationships.'

'That's what he told you?'

Aaron shrugged. 'That was my life. My brothers went to boarding school, I went to boot camp—military school starting at age seven. They had skiing and beach holidays. I went to training courses and had extra lessons. It was the price of being the oldest son.'

'But that's awful.'

'It is what it is. In any case, I idolised my father. I wanted to be like him: confident, in control, powerful.' He paused, his expression darkening. 'And then he died and I discovered it was all a lie.'

What I didn't like was being lied to. Over and over again, so my whole life was built on nothing but deception. Now she was starting to understand why he had said that.

'How was it a lie?' she asked quietly.

'He wasn't in control at all. The business was bankrupt and he'd given away money and shares to a bunch of mistresses—one in particular who took everything she could.' Bitterness roughened his voice. 'I promised myself I would never be like that. Never let a woman—or anyone—take my focus away from the business. Never be weak.'

Zoe sat back against the bench, realisation rushing through her. 'And when I asked you not to take that phone call, that's what you felt you were doing.'

'Not just the phone call. Everything—asking you to move in with me, to marry me, going to St Julian's to see you and be with you… In that moment it all felt like weakness.'

She blinked, her throat tightening. 'I see.'

'I don't think you do.' Aaron took her hand. 'I've been fighting weakness all my life, Zoe, trying to be strong, to seem strong. I never told anyone about the company's troubles, not even my brothers. I took it all on myself when I was twenty-one, which in retrospect was a ridiculous thing to do.' He shook his head. 'And today, when I left my office for the last time, I realised I felt relief. I'm glad to be shot of it all, to finally be free. To be free to be weak.'

'You could never be weak, Aaron,' Zoe whispered. 'You're the strongest man I know.'

'I'm weak with love,' he said. 'I'm in love with you, and it took me a long time to realise it. To accept it. Maybe I fell in love with you the first time you stole my phone.'

She laughed, the sound wobbly. 'I doubt it.'

'But I love you. And I'm not afraid of it now.' He

paused, squeezing her fingers. 'I can only ask you to forgive me for treating you so terribly. I knew you'd been hurt before and I acted just the same. I'm so sorry, Zoe.'

Her throat was so tight now she could barely speak, and yet her heart was full, so wonderfully full. 'I forgive you,' she whispered.

'And do you think you could take another chance on me? This is new territory for me, Zoe, and I admit it's still scary. The honesty, the emotion.' He gave her a shaky smile. 'The love. But I want to try…with you.'

Zoe swallowed. She could hardly believe she was hearing Aaron say these words. Yet she did believe them, so very much. And she want to try again, even though trying and loving were scary—for both of them. 'I love you,' she said softly. 'And, yes, I want to try with you. I want to more than try, Aaron. I want this to work.'

'It will work,' he promised as he took her in his arms. 'As long as you give me lots of chances to make mistakes and say sorry.'

She smiled as he kissed her. 'I promise,' she said. She kissed him back, stopping as his phone buzzed in his pocket. 'Are you going to get that?' she asked, and he smiled.

'Not a chance,' he answered, and deepened the kiss.

EPILOGUE

Three years later

ZOE STOOD NEXT to Aaron in the church and watched with a swell of both love and pride as he cradled their tiny daughter. Camilla Anne Bryant was three months old, and today was her christening.

Summer sunshine spilled into the church, gilding Aaron's hair in gold. Zoe's gaze moved from her husband—they'd been married a year ago—to the other couples in the room. Luke and Aurelie stood next to Aaron, their fingers laced. They hadn't yet started a family, but Zoe knew they were thinking about it. Love brimmed over in both of their eyes, and as Aaron handed Camilla to the minister she saw them exchange a small, secret smile.

She turned to look at Millie and Chase, who also stood together, Millie's hand resting protectively on the small swell of her baby bump. Zoe knew it had taken a long time for Millie to risk trying again, and she was so happy her sister and Chase were expecting a cousin for Camilla—this time a boy.

She let her gaze rest once more on her husband, the man she loved more than anyone, the man who had both changed himself and changed her. He must have felt her gaze on him, for he lifted his head and smiled. She knew he was thinking what a miracle this was, to have them all together, united, happy. And Camilla was a miracle; it had taken four attempts at IVF before Zoe had fallen pregnant but the heartache and frustrated hope had finally turned to joy.

Stepping forward to take her husband's hand, Zoe knew she had everything she'd ever wanted.

* * * * *

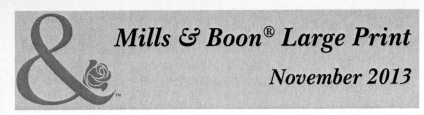

Mills & Boon® Large Print
November 2013

HIS MOST EXQUISITE CONQUEST
Emma Darcy

ONE NIGHT HEIR
Lucy Monroe

HIS BRAND OF PASSION
Kate Hewitt

THE RETURN OF HER PAST
Lindsay Armstrong

THE COUPLE WHO FOOLED THE WORLD
Maisey Yates

PROOF OF THEIR SIN
Dani Collins

IN PETRAKIS'S POWER
Maggie Cox

A COWBOY TO COME HOME TO
Donna Alward

HOW TO MELT A FROZEN HEART
Cara Colter

THE CATTLEMAN'S READY-MADE FAMILY
Michelle Douglas

WHAT THE PAPARAZZI DIDN'T SEE
Nicola Marsh

1013 Rom LP

Mills & Boon® Large Print
December 2013

THE BILLIONAIRE'S TROPHY
Lynne Graham

PRINCE OF SECRETS
Lucy Monroe

A ROYAL WITHOUT RULES
Caitlin Crews

A DEAL WITH DI CAPUA
Cathy Williams

IMPRISONED BY A VOW
Annie West

DUTY AT WHAT COST?
Michelle Conder

THE RINGS THAT BIND
Michelle Smart

A MARRIAGE MADE IN ITALY
Rebecca Winters

MIRACLE IN BELLAROO CREEK
Barbara Hannay

THE COURAGE TO SAY YES
Barbara Wallace

LAST-MINUTE BRIDESMAID
Nina Harrington

1113 Rom LP